SPIDERS WEB

Sandy Birch

Clive B. Canfield

"[illegible]"

Anna-Lisa Japscott

"PIPPA"

Barrie Fenton

"Elgin"

John Heyward

"HENRY"

[illegible]

"JEREMY"

Robert Crewe

"HUGO"

[illegible]

[illegible]

Keith [illegible]

"Jones?"

THE AGATHA CHRISTIE HOUR

By the same author

Sleeping Murder:
Miss Marple's Last Case
Curtain: Poirot's Last Case
Poirot's Early Cases
Postern of Fate
Elephants Can Remember
Nemesis
Passenger to Frankfurt
Hallowe'en Party
By the Pricking of My Thumbs
Endless Night
A Caribbean Mystery
Third Girl
At Bertram's Hotel
The Mirror Crack'd from Side to Side
The Pale Horse
The Adventure of the Christmas Pudding
Cat Among the Pigeons
Ordeal by Innocence
4.50 From Paddington
Dead Man's Folly
Hickory Dickory Dock
A Pocket Full of Rye
After the Funeral
Mrs McGinty's Dead
Taken at the Flood
The ABC Murders
The Mysterious Affair at Styles
etc., etc.

The Greenway Collected Edition

The Murder of Roger Ackroyd
The Labours of Hercules
Crooked House
A Murder is Announced
Cards on the Table
Why Didn't They Ask Evans?
Murder on the Orient Express
The Moving Finger
Lord Edgeware Dies
They Do It With Mirrors
Death on the Nile
They Came to Baghdad
Mystery of the Blue Train
Three Act Tragedy
Thirteen Problems
At Bertram's Hotel
Death in the Clouds
N or M?
Hercule Poirot's Christmas
Towards Zero
Murder at the Vicarage
The ABC Murders

Agatha Christie

THE AGATHA CHRISTIE HOUR

COLLINS
St James's Place London
1982

William Collins Sons & Co Ltd
London · Glasgow · Sydney · Auckland
Toronto · Johannesburg

Photoset in 11/13 pt Baskerville by
Rowland Phototypesetting Ltd
Bury St Edmunds, Suffolk
Made & printed in Great Britain by
William Collins Sons & Co Ltd, Glasgow

First published in 1982
by William Collins Sons & Co Ltd
Glasgow

ISBN: 0 00 231331 6

CONTENTS

The Fourth Man

Canon Parfitt panted a little. Running for trains was not much of a business for a man of his age. For one thing his figure was not what it was and with the loss of his slender silhouette went an increasing tendency to be short of breath. This tendency the Canon himself always referred to, with dignity, as '*My heart*, you know!'

He sank into the corner of the first-class carriage with a sigh of relief. The warmth of the heated carriage was most agreeable to him. Outside the snow was falling. Lucky to get a corner seat on a long night journey. Miserable business if you didn't. There ought to be a sleeper on this train.

The other three corners were already occupied, and noting this fact Canon Parfitt became aware that the man in the far corner was smiling at him in gentle recognition. He was a clean-shaven man with a quizzical face and hair just turning grey on the temples. His profession was so clearly the law that no one could have mistaken him for anything else for a moment. Sir George Durand was, indeed, a very famous lawyer.

'Well, Parfitt,' he remarked genially, 'you had a run for it, didn't you?'

'Very bad for my heart, I'm afraid,' said the Canon. 'Quite a coincidence meeting you, Sir George. Are you going far north?'

'Newcastle,' said Sir George laconically. 'By the way,' he added, 'do you know Dr Campbell Clark?'

The man sitting on the same side of the carriage as the Canon inclined his head pleasantly.

'We met on the platform,' continued the lawyer. 'Another coincidence.'

Canon Parfitt looked at Dr Campbell Clark with a good deal of interest. It was a name of which he had often heard. Dr Clark was in the forefront as a physician and mental specialist, and his last book, *The Problem of the Unconscious Mind*, had been the most discussed book of the year.

Canon Parfitt saw a square jaw, very steady blue eyes and reddish hair untouched by grey, but thinning rapidly. And he received also the impression of a very forceful personality.

By a perfectly natural association of ideas the Canon looked across to the seat opposite him, half-expecting to receive a glance of recognition there also, but the fourth occupant of the carriage proved to be a total stranger – a foreigner, the Canon fancied. He was a slight dark man, rather insignificant in appearance. Huddled in a big overcoat, he appeared to be fast asleep.

'Canon Parfitt of Bradchester?' inquired Dr Campbell Clark in a pleasant voice.

The Canon looked flattered. Those 'scientific sermons' of his had really made a great hit – especially since the Press had taken them up. Well, that was what the Church needed – good modern up-to-date stuff.

'I have read your book with great interest, Dr Campbell Clark,' he said. 'Though it's a bit technical here and there for me to follow.'

Durand broke in.

'Are you for talking or sleeping, Canon?' he asked. 'I'll confess at once that I suffer from insomnia and that therefore I'm in favour of the former.'

'Oh! certainly. By all means,' said the Canon. 'I seldom

sleep on these night journeys, and the book I have with me is a very dull one.'

'We are at any rate a representative gathering,' remarked the doctor with a smile. 'The Church, the Law, the Medical Profession.'

'Not much we couldn't give an opinion on between us, eh?' laughed Durand. 'The Church for the spiritual view, myself for the purely worldly and legal view, and you, doctor, with widest field of all, ranging from the purely pathological to the super-psychological! Between us three we should cover any ground pretty completely, I fancy.'

'Not so completely as you imagine, I think,' said Dr Clark. 'There's another point of view, you know, that you left out, and that's rather an important one.'

'Meaning?' queried the lawyer.

'The point of view of the Man in the Street.'

'Is that so important? Isn't the Man in the Street usually wrong?'

'Oh! almost always. But he has the thing that all expert opinion must lack – the personal point of view. In the end, you know, you can't get away from personal relationships. I've found that in my profession. For every patient who comes to me genuinely ill, at least five come who have nothing whatever the matter with them except an inability to live happily with the inmates of the same house. They call it everything – from housemaid's knee to writer's cramp, but it's all the same thing, the raw surface produced by mind rubbing against mind.'

'You have a lot of patients with "nerves", I suppose,' the Canon remarked disparagingly. His own nerves were excellent.

'Ah! and what do you mean by that?' The other swung round on him, quick as a flash. 'Nerves! People use that word and laugh after it, just as you did. "Nothing the matter with so and so," they say. "Just nerves." But, good God, man, you've got the crux of everything there! You can get at a mere bodily ailment and heal it. But at this day we know very little more about the obscure causes of the hundred and one forms of nervous disease than we did in – well, the reign of Queen Elizabeth!'

'Dear me,' said Canon Parfitt, a little bewildered by this onslaught. 'Is that so?'

'Mind you, it's a sign of grace,' Dr Campbell Clark went on. 'In the old days we considered man a simple animal, body and soul – with stress laid on the former.'

'Body, soul and spirit,' corrected the clergyman mildly.

'Spirit?' The doctor smiled oddly. 'What do you parsons mean exactly by spirit? You've never been very clear about it, you know. All down the ages you've funked an exact definition.'

The Canon cleared his throat in preparation for speech, but to his chagrin he was given no opportunity. The doctor went on.

'Are we even sure the word is spirit – might it not be *spirits*?'

'Spirits?' Sir George Durand questioned, his eyebrows raised quizzically.

'Yes.' Campbell Clark's gaze transferred itself to him. He leaned forward and tapped the other man lightly on the breast. 'Are you so sure,' he said gravely, 'that there is only one occupant of this structure – for that is all it is, you know – this desirable residence to be let furnished – for seven, twenty-one, forty-one, seventy-one – whatever it may be! – years? And in the end the tenant moves his things out – little by little – and then goes out of the house altogether – and down comes the house, a mass of ruin and decay. You're the master of the house – we'll admit that, but aren't you ever conscious of the presence of others – soft-footed servants, hardly noticed, except for the work they do – work that you're not conscious of having done? Or friends – moods that take hold of you and make you, for the time being, a "different man" as the saying goes? You're the king of the castle, right enough, but be very sure the "dirty rascal" is there too.'

'My dear Clark,' drawled the lawyer. 'You make me positively uncomfortable. Is my mind really a battleground of conflicting personalities? Is that Science's latest?'

It was the doctor's turn to shrug his shoulders.

'Your body is,' he said drily. 'If the body, why not the mind?'

'Very interesting,' said Canon Parfitt. 'Ah! Wonderful science – wonderful science.'

And inwardly he thought to himself: "I can get a most arresting sermon out of that idea."

But Dr Campbell Clark had leant back again in his seat, his momentary excitement spent.

'As a matter of fact,' he remarked in a dry professional manner, 'it is a case of dual personality that takes me to Newcastle tonight. Very interesting case. Neurotic subject, of course. But quite genuine.'

'Dual personality,' said Sir George Durand thoughtfully. 'It's not so very rare, I believe. There's loss of memory as well, isn't there? I know the matter cropped up in a case in the Probate Court the other day.'

Dr Clark nodded.

'The classic case, of course,' he said, 'was that of Felicie Bault. You may remember hearing of it?'

'Of course,' said Canon Parfitt. 'I remember reading about it in the papers – but quite a long time ago – seven years at least.'

Dr Campbell Clark nodded.

'That girl became one of the most famous figures in France. Scientists from all over the world came to see her. She had no less than four distinct personalities. They were known as Felicie 1, Felicie 2, Felicie 3, etc.'

'Wasn't there some suggestion of deliberate trickery?' asked Sir George alertly.

'The personalities of Felicie 3 and Felicie 4 were a little

open to doubt,' admitted the doctor. 'But the main facts remain. Felicie Bault was a Brittany peasant girl. She was the third of a family of five, the daughter of a drunken father and a mentally defective mother. In one of his drinking bouts the father strangled the mother and was, if I remember rightly, transported for life. Felicie was then five years of age. Some charitable people interested themselves in the children and Felicie was brought up and educated by an English maiden lady who had a kind of home for destitute children. She could make very little of Felicie, however. She describes the girl as abnormally slow and stupid, only taught to read and write with the greatest difficulty and clumsy with her hands. This lady, Miss Slater, tried to fit the girl for domestic service, and did indeed find her several places when she was of an age to take them. But she never stayed long anywhere owing to her stupidity and also her intense laziness.'

The doctor paused for a minute, and the Canon, re-crossing his legs, and arranging his travelling rug more closely round him, was suddenly aware that the man opposite him had moved very slightly. His eyes, which had formerly been shut, were now open, and something in them, something mocking and indefinable, startled the worthy Canon. It was as though the man were listening and gloating secretly over what he heard.

'There is a photograph taken of Felicie Bault at the age of seventeen,' continued the doctor. 'It shows her as a loutish peasant girl, heavy of build. There is nothing in that picture to indicate that she was soon to be one of the most famous persons in France.

'Five years later, when she was 22, Felicie Bault had a severe nervous illness, and on recovery the strange phenomena began to manifest themselves. The following are facts attested to by many eminent scientists. The personality called Felicie 1 was indistinguishable from the Felicie Bault of the last twenty-two years. Felicie 1 wrote French badly and haltingly, she spoke no foreign languages and was unable to play the piano. Felicie 2, on the contrary, spoke Italian fluently and German moderately. Her handwriting was quite dissimilar to that of Felicie 1, and she wrote fluent and expressive French. She could discuss politics and art and she was passionately fond of playing the piano. Felicie 3 had many points in common with Felicie 2. She was intelligent and apparently well educated, but in moral character she was a total contrast. She appeared, in fact, an utterly depraved creature – but depraved in a Parisian and not a provincial way. She knew all the Paris *argot*, and the expressions of the chic *demi monde*. Her language was filthy and she would rail against religion and so-called "good people" in the most blasphemous terms. Finally there was Felicie 4 – a dreamy, almost half-witted creature, distinctly pious and professedly clairvoyant, but this fourth personality was very unsatisfactory and elusive and has been sometimes thought to be a deliberate trickery on the part of Felicie 3 – a kind of joke played by her on a credulous public. I may say that (with the possible exception of Felicie 4) each personality was distinct and separate and had no knowledge of the others. Felicie 2 was undoubtedly the most predominant and would last sometimes for a fortnight at a time, then Felicie 1 would appear abruptly for a day or two. After that, perhaps, Felicie 3 or 4, but the two latter seldom remained in command for more than a few hours. Each change was accompanied by severe headache and heavy sleep, and in each case there was complete loss of memory of the other states, the personality in question taking up life where she had left it, unconscious of the passage of time.'

'Remarkable,' murmured the Canon. 'Very remarkable. As yet we know next to nothing of the marvels of the universe.'

'We know that there are some very astute impostors in it,' remarked the lawyer drily.

'The case of Felicie Bault was investigated by lawyers as well as by doctors and scientists,' said Dr Campbell Clark quickly. 'Maitre Quimbellier, you remember, made the most thorough investigation and confirmed the views of the scientists. And after all, why should it surprise us so much? We come across the double-yolked egg, do we not? And the twin banana? Why not the double soul – or in this case the quadruple soul – in the single body?'

'The double soul?' protested the Canon.

Dr Campbell Clark turned his piercing blue eyes on him.

'What else can we call it? That is to say – if the personality is the soul?'

'It is a good thing such a state of affairs is only in the nature of a "freak",' remarked Sir George. 'If the case were common, it would give rise to pretty complications.'

'The condition is, of course quite abnormal,' agreed the doctor. 'It was a great pity that a longer study could not have been made, but all that was put an end to by Felicie's unexpected death.'

'There was something queer about that, if I remember rightly,' said the lawyer slowly.

Dr Campbell Clark nodded.

'A most unaccountable business. The girl was found one morning dead in bed. She had clearly been strangled. But to everyone's stupefaction it was presently proved beyond doubt that she had actually strangled herself. The marks on her neck were those of her own fingers. A method of suicide which, though not physically impossible, must have necessitated terrific muscular strength and almost superhuman will power. What had driven the girl to such straits has never been found out. Of course her mental balance must always have been precarious. Still, there it is. The curtain has been rung down for ever on the mystery of Felicie Bault.'

It was then that the man in the far corner laughed.

The other three men jumped as though shot. They had totally forgotten the existence of the fourth amongst them. As they stared towards the place where he sat, still huddled in his overcoat, he laughed again.

'You must excuse me, gentlemen,' he said, in perfect English that had, nevertheless, a foreign flavour.

He sat up, displaying a pale face with a small jet-black moustache.

'Yes, you must excuse me,' he said, with a mock bow. 'But really! in science, is the last word ever said?'

'You know something of the case we have been discussing?' asked the doctor courteously.

'Of the case? No. But I knew her.'

'Felicie Bault?'

'Yes. And Annette Ravel also. You have not heard of Annette Ravel, I see? And yet the story of the one is the story of the other. Believe me, you know nothing of Felicie Bault if you do not also know the history of Annette Ravel.'

He drew out a watch and looked at it.

'Just half an hour before the next stop. I have time to tell you the story – that is, if you care to hear it?'

'Please tell it to us,' said the doctor quietly.

'Delighted,' said the Canon. 'Delighted.'

Sir George Durand merely composed himself in an attitude of keen attention.

'My name, gentlemen,' began their strange travelling companion, 'is Raoul Letardeau. You have spoken just now of an English lady, Miss Slater, who interested herself in works of charity. I was born in that Brittany fishing village and when my parents were both killed in a railway accident it was Miss Slater who came to the rescue and saved me from the equivalent of your English workhouse. There were some twenty children under her care, girls and boys. Amongst these children were Felicie Bault and Annette Ravel. If I cannot make you understand the personality of Annette, gentlemen, you will understand nothing. She was a child of what you call a "fille de joie" who had died of consumption, abandoned by her lover. The mother had been a dancer, and Annette, too, had the desire to dance. When I saw her first she was eleven years old, a little shrimp of a thing with eyes that alternately mocked and promised – a little creature all fire and life. And at once – yes, at once – she made me her slave. It was "Raoul, do this for me." "Raoul, do that for me." And me, I obeyed. Already I worshipped her, and she knew it.

'We would go down to the shore together, we three – for Felicie would come with us. And there Annette would pull off her shoes and stockings and dance on the sand. And then when she sank down breathless, she would tell us of what she meant to do and to be.

' "See you, I shall be famous. Yes, exceedingly famous. I will have hundreds and thousands of silk stockings – the finest silk. And I shall live in an exquisite apartment. All my lovers shall be young and handsome as well as being rich. And when I dance all Paris shall come to see me. They will yell and call and shout and go mad over my dancing. And in the winters I shall not dance. I shall go south to the sunlight. There are villas there with orange trees. I shall have one of them. I shall lie in the sun on silk cushions, eating oranges. As for you, Raoul, I will never forget you, however great and rich and famous I shall be. I will protect you and advance your career. Felicie here shall be my maid – no, her hands are too clumsy. Look at them, how large and coarse they are."

'Felicie would grow angry at that. And then Annette would go on teasing her.

' "She is so ladylike, Felicie – so elegant, so refined. She is a princess in disguise – ha, ha."

' "My father and mother were married, which is more than yours were,' Felicie would growl out spitefully.

' "Yes, and your father killed your mother. A pretty thing, to be a murderer's daughter."

' "Your father left your mother to rot," Felicie would rejoin.

' "Ah! yes.' Annette became thoughtful. "*Pauvre Maman.* One must keep strong and well. It is everything to keep strong and well."

'"I am as strong as a horse," Felicie boasted.

'And indeed she was. She had twice the strength of any other girl in the Home. And she was never ill.

'But she was stupid, you comprehend, stupid like a brute beast. I often wondered why she followed Annette round as she did. It was, with her, a kind of fascination. Sometimes, I think, she actually hated Annette, and indeed Annette was not kind to her. She jeered at her slowness and stupidity, and baited her in front of the others. I have seen Felicie grow quite white with rage. Sometimes I have thought that she would fasten her fingers round Annette's neck and choke the life out of her. She was not nimble-witted enough to reply to Annette's taunts, but she did learn in time to make one retort which never failed. That was a reference to her own health and strength. She had learned (what I had always known) that Annette envied her her strong physique, and she struck instinctively at the weak spot in her enemy's armour.

'One day Annette came to me in great glee.

'"Raoul," she said. "We shall have fun today with that stupid Felicie. We shall die of laughing."

'"What are you going to do?"

'"Come behind the little shed, and I will tell you."

'It seemed that Annette had got hold of some book. Part of it she did not understand, and indeed the whole thing was much over her head. It was an early work on hypnotism.

'"A bright object, they say. The brass knob of my bed, it twirls round. I made Felicie look at it last night. 'Look at it steadily,' I said. 'Do not take your eyes off it.' And then I twirled it. Raoul, I was frightened. Her eyes looked so queer – so queer. 'Felicie, you will do what I say always,' I said. 'I will do what you say always, Annette,' she answered. And then – and then – I said: 'Tomorrow you will bring a tallow candle out into the playground at twelve o'clock and start to eat it. And if anyone asks you, you will say that it is the best *galette* you ever tasted.' Oh! Raoul, think of it!"

'"But she'll never do such a thing," I objected.

'"The book says so. Not that I can quite believe it – but, oh! Raoul, if the book is all true, how we shall amuse ourselves!"

'I, too, thought the idea very funny. We passed word round to the comrades and at twelve o'clock we were all in the playground. Punctual to the minute, out came Felicie with a stump of candle in her hand. Will you believe me, Messieurs, she began solemnly to nibble at it? We were all in hysterics! Every now and then one or other of the children would go up to her and say solemnly: "It is good, what you eat there, eh, Felicie?" And she would answer. "But, yes, it is the best *galette* I ever tasted." And then we would shriek with laughter. We laughed at last so loud that the noise seemed to wake up Felicie to a realization of what she was doing. She blinked her eyes in a puzzled way, looked at the candle, then at us. She passed her hand over her forehead.

'"But what is it that I do here?" she muttered.

'"You are eating a candle," we screamed.

'"*I* made you do it. *I* made you do it," cried Annette, dancing about.

'Felicie stared for a moment. Then she went slowly up to Annette.

'"So it was you – it is you who have made me ridiculous? I seem to remember. Ah! I will kill you for this."

'She spoke in a very quiet tone, but Annette rushed suddenly away and hid behind me.

'"Save me, Raoul! I am afraid of Felicie. It was only a joke, Felicie. Only a joke."

'"I do not like these jokes," said Felicie. "You understand? I hate you. I hate you all."

'She suddenly burst out crying and rushed away.

'Annette was, I think, scared by the result of her experiment, and did not try to repeat it. But from that day on, her ascendancy over Felicie seemed to grow stronger.

'Felicie, I now believe, always hated her, but nevertheless

she could not keep away from her. She used to follow Annette around like a dog.

'Soon after that, Messieurs, employment was found for me, and I only came to the Home for occasional holidays. Annette's desire to become a dancer was not taken seriously, but she developed a very pretty singing voice as she grew older and Miss Slater consented to her being trained as a singer.

'She was not lazy, Annette. She worked feverishly, without rest. Miss Slater was obliged to prevent her doing too much. She spoke to me once about her.

' "You have always been fond of Annette," she said. "Persuade her not to work too hard. She has a little cough lately that I do not like."

'My work took me far afield soon afterwards. I received one or two letters from Annette at first, but then came silence. For five years after that I was abroad.

'Quite by chance, when I returned to Paris, my attention was caught by a poster advertizing Annette Ravelli with a picture of the lady. I recognized her at once. That night I went to the theatre in question. Annette sang in French and Italian. On the stage she was wonderful. Afterwards I went to her dressing-room. She received me at once.

' "Why, Raoul," she cried, stretching out her whitened hands to me. "This is splendid. Where have you been all these years?"

'I would have told her, but she did not really want to listen.

' "You see, I have very nearly arrived!"

'She waved a triumphant hand round the room filled with bouquets.

' "The good Miss Slater must be proud of your success."

' "That old one? No, indeed. She designed me, you know, for the Conservatoire. Decorous concert singing. But me, I am an artist. It is here, on the variety stage, that I can express myself."

'Just then a handsome middle-aged man came in. He was very distinguished. By his manner I soon saw that he was Annette's protector. He looked sideways at me, and Annette explained.

'"A friend of my infancy. He passes through Paris, sees my picture on a poster *et voilà*!"

'The man was then very affable and courteous. In my presence he produced a ruby and diamond bracelet and clasped it on Annette's wrist. As I rose to go, she threw me a glance of triumph and a whisper.

'"I arrive, do I not? You see? All the world is before me."

'But as I left the room, I heard her cough, a sharp dry cough. I knew what it meant, that cough. It was the legacy of her consumptive mother.

'I saw her next two years later. She had gone for refuge to Miss Slater. Her career had broken down. She was in a state of advanced consumption for which the doctors said nothing could be done.

'Ah! I shall never forget her as I saw her then! She was lying in a kind of shelter in the garden. She was kept outdoors night and day. Her cheeks were hollow and flushed, her eyes bright and feverish and she coughed repeatedly.

'She greeted me with a kind of desperation that startled me.

'"It is good to see you, Raoul. You know what they say – that I may not get well? They say it behind my back, you understand. To me they are soothing and consolatory. But it is not true, Raoul, it is not true! I shall not permit myself to die. Die? With beautiful life stretching in front of me? It is the will to live that matters. All the great doctors say that nowadays. I am not one of the feeble ones who let go. Already I feel myself infinitely better – infinitely better, do you hear?"

'She raised herself on her elbow to drive her words home, then fell back, attacked by a fit of coughing that racked her thin body.

'"The cough – it is nothing," she gasped. "And hæmorrhages do not frighten me. I shall surprise the doctors. It is the will that counts. Remember, Raoul, I am going to live."

'It was pitiful, you understand, pitiful.

'Just then, Felicie Bault came out with a tray. A glass of hot milk. She gave it to Annette and watched her drink it with an expression that I could not fathom. There was a kind of smug satisfaction in it.

'Annette too caught the look. She flung the glass down angrily, so that it smashed to bits.

'"You see her? That is how she always looks at me. She is glad I am going to die! Yes, she gloats over it. She who is well and strong. Look at her, never a day's illness, that one! And all for nothing. What good is that great carcass of hers to her? What can she make of it?"

'Felicie stooped and picked up the broken fragments of glass.

'"I do not mind what she says," she observed in a sing-song voice. "What does it matter? I am a respectable girl, I am. As for her. She will be knowing the fires of Purgatory before very long. I am a Christian, I say nothing."

'"You hate me," cried Annette. "You have always hated me. Ah! but I can charm you, all the same. I can make you do what I want. See now, if I ask you to, you would go down on your knees before me now on the grass."

'"You are absurd," said Felicie uneasily.

'"But, yes, you will do it. You will. To please me. Down on your knees. I ask it of you, I, Annette. Down on your knees, Felicie."

'Whether it was the wonderful pleading in her voice, or some deeper motive, Felicie obeyed. She sank slowly to her knees, her arms spread wide, her face vacant and stupid.

'Annette flung back her head and laughed – peal upon peal of laughter.

'"Look at her, with her stupid face! How ridiculous she looks. You can get up now, Felicie, thank you! It is of no use to scowl at me. I am your mistress. You have to do what I say."

'She lay back on her pillows exhausted. Felicie picked up the tray and moved slowly away. Once she looked back over her shoulder, and the smouldering resentment in her eyes startled me.

'I was not there when Annette died. But it was terrible, it seems. She clung to life. She fought against death like a madwoman. Again and again she gasped out: "I will not die – do you hear me? I will not die. I will live – live —"

'Miss Slater told me all this when I came to see her six months later.

' "My poor Raoul," she said kindly. "You loved her, did you not?"

' "Always – always. But of what use could I be to her? Let us not talk of it. She is dead – she so brilliant, so full of burning life. . . ."

'Miss Slater was a sympathetic woman. She went on to talk of other things. She was very worried about Felicie, so she told me. The girl had had a queer sort of nervous breakdown, and ever since she had been very strange in manner.

' "You know," said Miss Slater, after a momentary hesitation, "that she is learning the piano?"

'I did not know it, and was very much surprised to hear it. Felicie – learning the piano! I would have declared the girl would not know one note from another.

' "She has talent, they say," continued Miss Slater. "I can't understand it. I have always put her down as – well, Raoul, you know yourself, she was always a stupid girl."

'I nodded.

' "She is so strange in her manner sometimes – I really don't know what to make of it."

'A few minutes later I entered the Salle de Lecture. Felicie was playing the piano. She was playing the air that I had heard Annette sing in Paris. You understand, Messieurs, it gave me quite a turn. And then, hearing me, she broke off suddenly and looked round at me, her eyes full of mockery and intelligence. For a moment I thought—— Well, I will not tell you what I thought.

'"Tiens!" she said. "So it is you – *Monsieur* Raoul."

'I cannot describe the way she said it. To Annette I had never ceased to be Raoul. But Felicie, since we had met as grown-ups, always addressed me as *Monsieur* Raoul. But the way she said it now was different – as though the *Monsieur*, slightly stressed, was somehow very amusing.

'"Why, Felicie," I stammered. "You look quite different today."

'"Do I?" she said reflectively. "It is odd, that. But do not be so solemn Raoul – decidedly I shall call you Raoul – did we not play together as children? – Life was made for laughter. Let us talk of the poor Annette – she who is dead and buried. Is she in Purgatory, I wonder, or where?"

'And she hummed a snatch of song – untunefully enough, but the words caught my attention.

'"Felicie," I cried. "You speak Italian?"

'"Why not, Raoul? I am not as stupid as I pretend to be, perhaps." She laughed at my mystification.

'"I don't understand——" I began.

'"But I will tell you. I am a very fine actress, though no one suspects it. I can play many parts – and play them very well."

'She laughed again and ran quickly out of the room before I could stop her.

'I saw her again before I left. She was asleep in an armchair. She was snoring heavily. I stood and watched her, fascinated, yet repelled. Suddenly she woke with a start. Her eyes, dull and lifeless, met mine.

'"Monsieur Raoul," she muttered mechanically.

'"Yes, Felicie, I am going now. Will you play to me again before I go?"

'"I? Play? You are laughing at me, Monsieur Raoul."

'"Don't you remember playing to me this morning?"

'She shook her head.

'"I play? How can a poor girl like me play?"

'She paused for a minute as though in thought, then beckoned me nearer.

'"Monsieur Raoul, there are strange things going on in this house! They play tricks upon you. They alter the clocks. Yes, yes, I know what I am saying. And it is all her doing."

'"Whose doing?" I asked, startled.

'"That Annette's. That wicked one's. When she was alive she always tormented me. Now that she is dead, she comes back from the dead to torment me."

'I stared at Felicie. I could see now that she was in an extremity of terror, her eyes staring from her head.

'"She is bad, that one. She is bad, I tell you. She would take the bread from your mouth, the clothes from your back, *the soul from your body*. . . ."

'She clutched me suddenly.

'"I am afraid, I tell you – afraid. I hear her voice – not in my ear – no, not in my ear. Here, in my head——" She tapped her forehead. "She will drive me away – drive me away altogether, and then what shall I do, what will become of me?"

'Her voice rose almost to a shriek. She had in her eyes the look of the terrified brute beast at bay . . .

'Suddenly she smiled, a pleasant smile, full of cunning, with something in it that made me shiver.

'"If it should come to it, Monsieur Raoul, I am very strong with my hands – very strong with my hands."

'I had never noticed her hands particularly before. I looked at them now and shuddered in spite of myself. Squat brutal fingers, and as Felicie had said, terribly strong. . . . I cannot explain to you the nausea that swept over me. With hands such as these her father must have strangled her mother. . . .'

'That was the last time I ever saw Felicie Bault. Immediately afterwards I went abroad – to South America. I returned from there two years after her death. Something I had read in the newspapers of her life and sudden death. I have heard fuller details tonight – from you – gentlemen! Felicie 3 and Felicie 4 – I wonder? She was a good actress, you know!'

The train suddenly slackened speed. The man in the corner sat erect and buttoned his overcoat more closely.

'What is your theory?' asked the lawyer, leaning forward.

'I can hardly believe——' began Canon Parfitt, and stopped.

The doctor said nothing. He was gazing steadily at Raoul Lepardeau.

'The clothes from your back, the soul from your body,' quoted the Frenchman lightly. He stood up. 'I say to you, Messieurs, that the history of Felicie Bault is the history of Annette Ravel. You did not know her, gentlemen. I did. *She was very fond of life. . . .'*

His hand on the door, ready to spring out, he turned suddenly and bending down tapped Canon Parfitt on the chest.

'M. le docteur over there, he said just now, that all *this'* – his hand smote the Canon's stomach, and the Canon winced – 'was only a residence. Tell me, if you find a burglar in your house what do you do? Shoot him, do you not?'

'No,' cried the Canon. 'No, indeed – I mean – not in this country.'

But he spoke the last words to empty air. The carriage door banged.

The clergyman, the lawyer and the doctor were alone. The fourth corner was vacant.

The Case of the Discontented Soldier

Major Wilbraham hesitated outside the door of Mr Parker Pyne's office to read, not for the first time, the advertisement from the morning paper which had brought him there. It was simple enough:

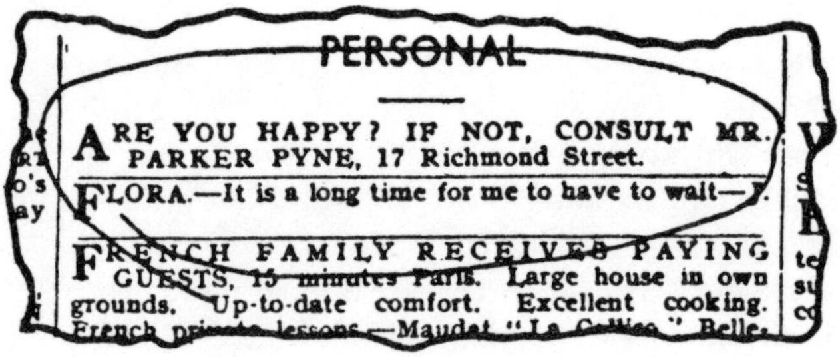
PERSONAL

ARE YOU HAPPY? IF NOT, CONSULT MR. PARKER PYNE, 17 Richmond Street.

FLORA.—It is a long time for me to have to wait—J.

FRENCH FAMILY RECEIVES PAYING GUESTS, 15 minutes Paris. Large house in own grounds. Up-to-date comfort. Excellent cooking.

The major took a deep breath and abruptly plunged through the swing door leading to the outer office. A plain young woman looked up from her typewriter and glanced at him inquiringly.

'Mr Parker Pyne?' said Major Wilbraham, blushing.

'Come this way, please.'

He followed her into an inner office – into the presence of the bland Mr Parker Pyne.

'Good-morning,' said Mr Pyne. 'Sit down, won't you? And now tell me what I can do for you.'

'My name is Wilbraham——' began the other.

'Major? Colonel?' said Mr Pyne.

'Major.'

'Ah! And recently returned from abroad? India? East Africa?'

'East Africa.'

'A fine country, I believe. Well, so you are home again – and you don't like it. Is that the trouble?'

'You're absolutely right. Though how you knew——'

Mr Parker Pyne waved an impressive hand. 'It is my business to know. You see, for thirty-five years of my life I have been engaged in the compiling of statistics in a government office. Now I have retired and it has occurred to me to use the experience I have gained in a novel fashion. It is all so simple. Unhappiness can be classified under five main heads – no more, I assure you. Once you know the cause of a malady, the remedy should not be impossible.

'I stand in the place of the doctor. The doctor first diagnoses the patient's disorder, then he recommends a course of treatment. There are cases where no treatment can be of any avail. If that is so, I say quite frankly that I can do nothing about it. But if I undertake a case, the cure is practically guaranteed.

'I can assure you, Major Wilbraham, that ninety-six per cent of retired empire builders – as I call them – are unhappy. They exchange an active life, a life full of responsibility, a life of possible danger, for – what? Straitened means, a dismal climate and a general feeling of being a fish out of water.'

'All you've said is true,' said the major. 'It's the boredom I object to. The boredom and the endless tittle-tattle about petty village matters. But what can I do about it? I've got a little money besides my pension. I've a nice cottage near Cobham. I can't afford to hunt or shoot or fish. I'm not married. My neighbours are all pleasant folk, but they've no ideas beyond this island.'

'The long and short of the matter is that you find life tame,' said Mr Parker Pyne.

'Damned tame.'

'You would like excitement, possibly danger?' asked Mr Pyne.

The soldier shrugged. 'There's no such thing in this tin-pot country.'

'I beg your pardon,' said Mr Pyne seriously. 'There you are wrong. There is plenty of danger, plenty of excitement, here in London if you know where to go for it. You have seen only the surface of our English life, calm, pleasant. But there is another side. If you wish it, I can show you that other side.'

Major Wilbraham regarded him thoughtfully. There was something reassuring about Mr Pyne. He was large, not to say fat; he had a bald head of noble proportions, strong glasses and little twinkling eyes. And he had an aura – an aura of dependability.

'I should warn you, however,' continued Mr Pyne, 'that there is an element of risk.'

The soldier's eye brightened. 'That's all right,' he said. Then, abruptly: 'And – your fees?'

'My fee,' said Mr Pyne, 'is fifty pounds, payable in advance. If in a month's time you are still in the same state of boredom, I will refund your money.'

Wilbraham considered. 'Fair enough,' he said at last. 'I agree. I'll give you a cheque now.'

The transaction was completed. Mr Parker Pyne pressed a buzzer on his desk.

'It is now one o'clock,' he said. 'I am going to ask you to take a young lady out to lunch.' The door opened. 'Ah, Madeleine, my dear, let me introduce Major Wilbraham, who is going to take you out to lunch.'

Wilbraham blinked slightly, which was hardly to be wondered at. The girl who entered the room was dark, languorous, with wonderful eyes and long black lashes, a perfect complexion and a voluptuous scarlet mouth. Her exquisite clothes set off the swaying grace of her figure. From head to foot she was perfect.

'Er – delighted,' said Major Wilbraham.

'Miss de Sara,' said Mr Parker Pyne.

'How very kind of you,' murmured Madeleine de Sara.

'I have your address here,' announced Mr Parker Pyne. 'Tomorrow morning you will receive my further instructions.'

Major Wilbraham and the lovely Madeleine departed.

It was three o'clock when Madeleine returned.

Mr Parker Pyne looked up. 'Well?' he demanded.

Madeleine shook her head. 'Scared of me,' she said. 'Thinks I'm a vamp.'

'I thought as much,' said Mr Parker Pyne. 'You carried out my instructions?'

'Yes. We discussed the occupants of the other tables freely. The type he likes is fair-haired, blue-eyed, slightly anæmic, not too tall.'

'That should be easy,' said Mr Pyne. 'Get me Schedule B and let me see what we have in stock at present.' He ran his finger down a list, finally stopping at a name. 'Freda Clegg. Yes, I think Freda Clegg will do excellently. I had better see Mrs Oliver about it.'

The next day Major Wilbraham received a note, which read:

> On Monday morning next at eleven o'clock go to Eaglemont, Friars Lane, Hampstead, and ask for Mr Jones. You will represent yourself as coming from the Guava Shipping Company.

Obediently on the following Monday (which happened to be Bank Holiday), Major Wilbraham set out for Eaglemont, Friars Lane. He set out, I say, but he never got there. For before he got there, something happened.

All the world and his wife seemed to be on their way to Hampstead. Major Wilbraham got entangled in crowds, suffocated in the tube and found it hard to discover the whereabouts of Friars Lane.

Friars Lane was a cul-de-sac, a neglected road full of ruts, with houses on either side standing back from the road. They were largish houses which had seen better days and had been allowed to fall into disrepair.

Wilbraham walked along peering at the half-erased names on the gate-posts, when suddenly he heard something that made him stiffen to attention. It was a kind of gurgling, half-choked cry.

It came again and this time it was faintly recognizable as the word 'Help!' It came from inside the wall of the house he was passing.

Without a moment's hesitation, Major Wilbraham pushed open the rickety gate and sprinted noiselessly up the weed-covered drive. There in the shrubbery was a girl struggling in the grasp of two enormous Negroes. She was putting up a brave fight, twisting and turning and kicking. One Negro held his hand over her mouth in spite of her furious efforts to get her head free.

Intent on their struggle with the girl, neither of the blacks had noticed Wilbraham's approach. The first they knew of it was when a violent punch on the jaw sent the man who was covering the girl's mouth reeling backwards. Taken by surprise, the other man relinquished his hold of the girl and turned. Wilbraham was ready for him. Once again his fist shot out, and the Negro reeled backwards and fell. Wilbraham turned on the other man, who was closing in behind him.

But the two men had had enough. The second one rolled over, sat up; then, rising, he made a dash for the gate. His companion followed suit. Wilbraham started after them, but changed his mind and turned towards the girl, who was leaning against a tree, panting.

'Oh, thank you!' she gasped. 'It was terrible.'

Major Wilbraham saw for the first time who it was he had

rescued so opportunely. She was a girl of about twenty-one or two, fair-haired and blue-eyed, pretty in a rather colourless way.

'If you hadn't come!' she gasped.

'There, there,' said Wilbraham soothingly. 'It's all right now. I think, though, that we'd better get away from here. It's possible those fellows might come back.

A faint smile came to the girl's lips. 'I don't think they will – not after the way you hit them. Oh, it was splendid of you!'

Major Wilbraham blushed under the warmth of her glance of admiration. 'Nothin' at all,' he said indistinctly. 'All in a day's work. Lady being annoyed. Look here, if you take my arm, can you walk? It's been a nasty shock, I know.'

'I'm all right now,' said the girl. However, she took the proffered arm. She was still rather shaky. She glanced behind her at the house as they emerged through the gate. 'I can't understand it,' she murmured. 'That's clearly an empty house.'

'It's empty, right enough,' agreed the major, looking up at the shuttered windows and general air of decay.

'And yet it *is* Whitefriars.' She pointed to a half-obliterated name on the gate. 'And Whitefriars was the place I was to go.'

'Don't worry about anything now,' said Wilbraham. 'In a minute or two we'll be able to get a taxi. Then we'll drive somewhere and have a cup of coffee.'

At the end of the lane they came out into a more frequented street, and by good fortune a taxi had just set down a fare at one of the houses. Wilbraham hailed it, gave an address to the driver and they got in.

'Don't try to talk,' he admonished his companion. 'Just lie back. You've had a nasty experience.'

She smiled at him gratefully.

'By the way – er – my name is Wilbraham.'

'Mine is Clegg – Freda Clegg.'

Ten minutes later, Freda was sipping hot coffee and

looking gratefully across a small table at her rescuer.

'It seems like a dream,' she said. 'A bad dream.' She shuddered. 'And only a short while ago I was wishing for something to happen – anything! Oh, I don't like adventures.'

'Tell me how it happened.'

'Well, to tell you properly I shall have to talk a lot about myself, I'm afraid.'

'An excellent subject,' said Wilbraham, with a bow.

'I am an orphan. My father – he was a sea captain – died when I was eight. My mother died three years ago. I work in the city. I am with the Vacuum Gas Company – a clerk. One evening last week I found a gentleman waiting to see me when I returned to my lodgings. He was a lawyer, a Mr Reid from Melbourne.

'He was very polite and asked me several questions about my family. He explained that he had known my father many years ago. In fact, he had transacted some legal business for him. Then he told me the object of his visit. "Miss Clegg," he said, "I have reason to suppose that you might benefit as the result of a financial transaction entered into by your father several years before he died." I was very much surprised, of course.

' "It is unlikely that you would ever have heard anything of the matter," he explained. "John Clegg never took the affair seriously, I fancy. However, it has materialized unexpectedly, but I am afraid any claim you might put in would depend on your ownership of certain papers. These papers would be part of your father's estate, and of course it is possible that they have been destroyed as worthless. Have you kept any of your father's papers?"

'I explained that my mother had kept various things of my father's in an old sea chest. I had looked through it cursorily, but had discovered nothing of interest.

' "You would hardly be likely to recognize the importance of these documents, perhaps," he said, smiling.

'Well, I went to the chest, took out the few papers it contained and brought them to him. He looked at them, but said it was impossible to say off-hand what might or might not be connected with the matter in question. He would take them away with him and would communicate with me if anything turned up.

'By the last post on Saturday I received a letter from him in which he suggested that I come to his house to discuss the matter. He gave me the address: Whitefriars, Friars Lane, Hampstead. I was to be there at a quarter to eleven this morning.

'I was a little late finding the place. I hurried through the gate and up towards the house, when suddenly those two dreadful men sprang at me from the bushes. I hadn't time to cry out. One man put his hand over my mouth. I wrenched my head free and screamed for help. Luckily you heard me. If it hadn't been for you——' She stopped. Her looks were more eloquent than further words.

'Very glad I happened to be on the spot. By Gad, I'd like to get hold of those two brutes. You'd never seen them before, I suppose?'

She shook her head. 'What do you think it means?'

'Difficult to say. But one thing seems pretty sure. There's something some one wants among your father's papers. This man Reid told you a cock-and-bull story so as to get the opportunity of looking through them. Evidently what he wanted wasn't there.'

'Oh!' said Freda. 'I wonder. When I got home on Saturday I thought my things had been tampered with. To tell you the truth, I suspected my landlady of having pried about in my room out of curiosity. But now——'

'Depend upon it, that's it. Some one gained admission to your room and searched it, without finding what he was after. He suspected that you knew the value of this paper, whatever it was, and that you carried it about your person. So he planned this ambush. If you had it with you, it would have been taken from you. If not, you would have been held prisoner while he tried to make you tell where it was hidden.

'But what can it possibly *be*?' cried Freda.

'I don't know. But it must be something pretty good for him to go to this length.'

'It doesn't seem possible.'

'Oh, I don't know. Your father was a sailor. He went to out-of-the-way places. He might have come across something the value of which he never knew.'

'Do you really think so?' A pink flush of excitement showed in the girl's pale cheeks.

'I do indeed. The question is, what shall we do next? You don't want to go to the police, I suppose?'

'Oh, no, please.'

'I'm glad you say that. I don't see what good the police could do, and it would only mean unpleasantness for you. Now I suggest that you allow me to give you lunch somewhere and that I then accompany you back to your lodgings, so as to be sure you reach them safely. And then, we might have a look for the paper. Because, you know, it must be somewhere.'

'Father may have destroyed it himself.'

'He may, of course, but the other side evidently doesn't think so, and that looks hopeful for us.'

'What do you think it can be? Hidden treasure?'

'By jove, it might be!' exclaimed Major Wilbraham, all the boy in him rising joyfully to the suggestion. 'But now, Miss Clegg, lunch!'

They had a pleasant meal together. Wilbraham told Freda all about his life in East Africa. He described elephant hunts, and the girl was thrilled. When they had finished, he insisted on taking her home in a taxi.

Her lodgings were near Notting Hill Gate. On arriving there, Freda had a brief conversation with her landlady. She returned to Wilbraham and took him up to the second floor, where she had a tiny bedroom and sitting-room.

'It's exactly as we thought,' she said. 'A man came on Saturday morning to see about laying a new electric cable; he told her there was a fault in the wiring in my room. He was there some time.'

'Show me this chest of your father's,' said Wilbraham.

Freda showed him a brass-bound box. 'You see,' she said, raising the lid, 'it's empty.'

The soldier nodded thoughtfully. 'And there are no papers anywhere else?'

'I'm sure there aren't. Mother kept everything in here.'

Wilbraham examined the inside of the chest. Suddenly he uttered an exclamation. 'Here's a slit in the lining.' Carefully he inserted his hand, feeling about. A slight crackle rewarded him. 'Something's slipped down behind.'

In another minute he had drawn out his find. A piece of dirty paper folded several times. He smoothed it out on the table; Freda was looking over his shoulder. She uttered an exclamation of disappointment.

'It's just a lot of queer marks.'

'Why, the thing's in Swahili. *Swahili*, of all things!' cried Major Wilbraham. 'East African native dialect, you know.'

'How extraordinary!' said Freda. 'Can you read it, then?'

'Rather. But what an amazing thing.' He took the paper to the window.

'Is it anything?' asked Freda tremulously. Wilbraham read the thing through twice, and then came back to the girl. 'Well,' he said, with a chuckle, 'here's your hidden treasure, all right.'

'Hidden treasure? Not *really*? You mean Spanish gold – a sunken galleon – that sort of thing?'

'Not quite so romantic as that, perhaps. But it comes to the same thing. This paper gives the hiding-place of a cache of ivory.'

'Ivory?' said the girl, astonished.

'Yes. Elephants, you know. There's a law about the

number you're allowed to shoot. Some hunter got away with breaking that law on a grand scale. They were on his trail and he cached the stuff. There's a thundering lot of it – and this gives fairly clear directions how to find it. Look here, we'll have to go after this, you and I.'

'You mean there's really a lot of money in it?'

'Quite a nice little fortune for you.'

'But how did that paper come to be among my father's things?'

Wilbraham shrugged. 'Maybe the Johnny was dying or something. He may have written the thing down in Swahili for protection and given it to your father, who possibly had befriended him in some way. Your father, not being able to read it, attached no importance to it. That's only a guess on my part, but I dare say it's not far wrong.'

Freda gave a sigh. 'How frightfully exciting!'

'The thing is – what to do with the precious document,' said Wilbraham. 'I don't like leaving it here. They might come and have another look. I suppose you wouldn't entrust it to me?'

'Of course I would. But – mightn't it be dangerous for you?' she faltered.

'I'm a tough nut,' said Wilbraham grimly. 'You needn't worry about me.' He folded up the paper and put it in his pocket-book. 'May I come to see you tomorrow evening?' he asked. 'I'll have worked out a plan by then, and I'll look up the places on my map. What time do you get back from the city?'

'I get back about half-past six.'

'Capital. We'll have a powwow and then perhaps you'll let me take you out to dinner. We ought to celebrate. So long, then. Tomorrow at half-past six.'

Major Wilbraham arrived punctually on the following day. He rang the bell and inquired for Miss Clegg. A maid-servant had answered the door.

'Miss Clegg? She's out.'

'Oh!' Wilbraham did not like to suggest that he come in and wait. 'I'll call back presently,' he said.

He hung about in the street outside, expecting every minute to see Freda tripping towards him. The minutes passed. Quarter to seven. Seven. Quarter-past seven. Still no Freda. A feeling of uneasiness swept over him. He went back to the house and rang the bell again.

'Look here,' he said, 'I had an appointment with Miss Clegg at half-past six. Are you sure she isn't in or hasn't – er – left any message?'

'Are you Major Wilbraham?' asked the servant.

'Yes.'

'Then there's a note for you. It come by hand.

Wilbraham took it from her and tore it open. It ran as follows:

> Dear Major Wilbraham, – Something rather strange has happened. I won't write more now, but will you meet me at Whitefriars? Go there as soon as you get this.
>
> Yours sincerely,
>
> FREDA CLEGG.

Wilbraham drew his brows together as he thought rapidly. His hand drew a letter absent-mindedly from his pocket. It was to his tailor. 'I wonder,' he said to the maid-servant, 'if you could let me have a stamp.'

'I expect Mrs Parkins could oblige you.'

She returned in a moment with the stamp. It was paid for with a shilling. In another minute Wilbraham was walking towards the tube station, dropping the envelope in a box as he passed.

Freda's letter had made him most uneasy. What could have taken the girl, alone, to the scene of yesterday's sinister encounter?

He shook his head. Of all the foolish things to do! Had Reid reappeared? Had he somehow or other prevailed upon the girl to trust him? What had taken her to Hampstead?

He looked at his watch. Nearly half-past seven. She would have counted on his starting at half-past six. An hour late. Too much. If only she had had the sense to give him some hint.

The letter puzzled him. Somehow its independent tone was not characteristic of Freda Clegg.

It was ten minutes to eight when he reached Friars Lane. It was getting dark. He looked sharply about him; there was no one in sight. Gently he pushed the rickety gate so that it swung noiselessly on its hinges. The drive was deserted. The house was dark. He went up the path cautiously, keeping a look out from side to side. He did not intend to be caught by surprise.

Suddenly he stopped. Just for a minute a chink of light had shone through one of the shutters. The house was not empty. There was some one inside.

Softly Wilbraham slipped into the bushes and worked his way round to the back of the house. At last he found what he was looking for. One of the windows on the ground floor was unfastened. It was the window of a kind of scullery. He raised the sash, flashed a torch (he had bought it at a shop on the way over) around the deserted interior and climbed in.

Carefully he opened the scullery door. There was no sound. He flashed the torch once more. A kitchen – empty. Outside the kitchen were half a dozen steps and a door evidently leading to the front part of the house.

He pushed open the door and listened. Nothing. He slipped through. He was now in the front hall. Still there was no sound. There was a door to the right and a door to the left. He chose the right-hand door, listened for a time, then turned the handle. It gave. Inch by inch he opened the door and stepped inside.

Again he flashed the torch. The room was unfurnished and bare.

Just at that moment he heard a sound behind him, whirled

round – too late. Something came down on his head and he pitched forward into unconsciousness. . . .

How much time elapsed before he regained consciousness Wilbraham had no idea. He returned painfully to life, his head aching. He tried to move and found it impossible. He was bound with ropes.

His wits came back to him suddenly. He remembered now. He had been hit on the head.

A faint light from a gas jet high up on the wall showed him that he was in a small cellar. He looked around and his heart gave a leap. A few feet away lay Freda, bound like himself. Her eyes were closed, but even as he watched her anxiously, she sighed and they opened. Her bewildered gaze fell on him and joyous recognition leaped into them.

'You, too!' she said. 'What has happened?'

'I've let you down badly,' said Wilbraham. 'Tumbled headlong into the trap. Tell me, did you send me a note asking me to meet you here?'

'The girl's eyes opened in astonishment. '*I*? But you sent *me* one.'

'Oh, I sent you one, did I?'

'Yes. I got it at the office. It asked me to meet you here instead of at home.'

'Same method for both of us,' he groaned, and he explained the situation.

'I see,' said Freda. 'Then the idea was——'

'To get the paper. We must have been followed yesterday. That's how they got on to me.'

'And – have they got it?' asked Freda.

'Unfortunately, I can't feel and see,' said the soldier, regarding his bound hands ruefully.

And then they both started. For a voice spoke, a voice that seemed to come from the empty air.

'Yes, thank you,' it said. 'I've got it, all right. No mistake about that.'

The unseen voice made them both shiver.

'Mr Reid,' murmured Freda.

'Mr Reid is one of my names, my dear young lady,' said the voice. 'But only one of them. I have a great many. Now, I am sorry to say that you two have interfered with my plans – a thing I never allow. Your discovery of this house is a serious matter. You have not told the police about it yet, but you might do so in the future.

'I very much fear that I cannot trust you in the matter. You might promise – but promises are seldom kept. And, you see, this house is very useful to me. It is, you might say, my clearing house. The house from which there is no return. From here you pass on – elsewhere. You, I am sorry to say, are so passing on. Regrettable – but necessary.'

The voice paused for a brief second, then resumed: 'No bloodshed. I abhor bloodshed. My method is much simpler. And really not too painful, so I understand. Well, I must be getting along. Good-evening to you both.'

'Look here!' It was Wilbraham who spoke. 'Do what you like to me, but this young lady has done nothing – nothing. It can't hurt you to let her go.'

But there was no answer.

At that moment there came a cry from Freda. 'The water – the water!'

Wilbraham twisted himself painfully and followed the direction of her eyes. From a hole up near the ceiling a steady trickle of water was pouring in.

Freda gave a hysterical cry. 'They're going to drown us!'

The perspiration broke out on Wilbraham's brow. 'We're not done yet,' he said. 'We'll shout for help. Surely somebody will hear. Now, both together.'

They yelled and shouted at the top of their voices. Not till they were hoarse did they stop.

'No use, I'm afraid,' said Wilbraham sadly. 'We're too far underground and I expect the doors are muffled. After all, if we could be heard, I've no doubt that brute would have gagged us.'

'Oh!' cried Freda. 'And it's all my fault. I got you into this.'

'Don't worry about that, little girl. It's you I'm thinking about. I've been in tight corners before now and got out of them. Don't you lose heart. I'll get you out of this. We've plenty of time. At the rate that water's flowing in, it will be hours before the worst happens.'

'How wonderful you are!' said Freda. 'I've never met anybody like you – except in books.'

'Nonsense – just common sense. Now, I've got to loosen these infernal ropes.'

At the end of a quarter of an hour, by dint of straining and twisting, Wilbraham had the satisfaction of feeling that his bonds were appreciably loosened. He managed to bend his head down and his wrists up till he was able to attack the knots with his teeth.

Once his hands were free, the rest was only a matter of time. Cramped, stiff, but free, he bent over the girl. A minute later she also was free.

So far the water was only up to their ankles.

'And now,' said the soldier, 'to get out of here.'

The door of the cellar was up a few stairs. Major Wilbraham examined it.

'No difficulty here,' he said. 'Flimsy stuff. It will soon give at the hinges.' He set his shoulders to it and heaved.

There was the cracking of wood – a crash, and the door burst from its hinges.

Outside was a flight of stairs. At the top was another door – a very different affair – of solid wood, barred with iron.

'A bit more difficult, this,' said Wilbraham. 'Hallo, here's a piece of luck. It's unlocked.'

He pushed it open, peered round it, then beckoned the girl to come on. They emerged into a passage behind the kitchen. In another moment they were standing under the stars in Friars Lane.

'Oh!' Freda gave a little sob. 'Oh, how dreadful it's been!'

'My poor darling.' He caught her in his arms. 'You've been so wonderfully brave. Freda – darling angel – could you ever – I mean, would you – I love you, Freda. Will you marry me?'

After a suitable interval, highly satisfactory to both parties, Major Wilbraham said, with a chuckle:

'And what's more, we've still got the secret of the ivory cache.'

'But they took it from you!'

The major chuckled again. 'That's just what they didn't do! You see, I wrote out a spoof copy, and before joining you here tonight, I put the real thing in a letter I was sending to my tailor and posted it. They've got the spoof copy – and I wish them joy of it! Do you know what we'll do, sweetheart! We'll go to East Africa for our honeymoon and hunt out the cache.'

Mr Parker Pyne left his office and climbed two flights of stairs. Here in a room at the top of the house sat Mrs Oliver, the sensational novelist, now a member of Mr Pyne's staff.

Mr Parker Pyne tapped at the door and entered. Mrs Oliver sat at a table on which were a typewriter, several notebooks, a general confusion of loose manuscripts and a large bag of apples.

'A very good story, Mrs Oliver,' said Mr Parker Pyne genially.

'It went off well?' said Mrs Oliver. 'I'm glad.'

'That water-in-the-cellar business,' said Mr Parker Pyne. 'You don't think, on a future occasion, that something more original – perhaps?' He made the suggestion with proper diffidence.

Mrs Oliver shook her head and took an apple from the bag. 'I think not, Mr Pyne. You see, people are used to reading about such things. Water rising in a cellar, poison gas, et cetera. Knowing about it beforehand gives it an extra thrill when it happens to oneself. The public is conservative, Mr Pyne; it likes the old well-worn gadgets.'

'Well, you should know,' admitted Mr Parker Pyne, mindful of the authoress's forty-six successful works of fiction, all best sellers in England and America, and freely translated into French, German, Italian, Hungarian, Finnish, Japanese and Abyssinian. 'How about expenses?'

Mrs Oliver drew a paper towards her. 'Very moderate, on the whole. The two darkies, Percy and Jerry, wanted very little. Young Lorrimer, the actor, was willing to enact the part of Mr Reid for five guineas. The cellar speech was a phonograph record, of course.'

'Whitefriars has been extremely useful to me,' said Mr Pyne. 'I bought it for a song and it has already been the scene of eleven exciting dramas.'

'Oh, I forgot,' said Mrs Oliver. 'Johnny's wages. Five shillings.'

'Johnny?'

'Yes. The boy who poured the water from the watering cans through the hole in the wall.'

'Ah, yes. By the way, Mrs Oliver, how did you happen to know Swahili?'

'I didn't.'

'I see. The British Museum, perhaps?'

'No. Delfridge's Information Bureau.'

'How marvellous are the resources of modern commerce!' he murmured.

'The only thing that worries me,' said Mrs Oliver, 'is that those two young people won't find any cache when they get there.'

'One cannot have everything in this world,' said Mr Parker Pyne. 'They will have had a honeymoon.'

Mrs Wilbraham was sitting in a deck-chair. Her husband was writing a letter. 'What's the date, Freda?'

'The sixteenth.'

'The sixteenth. By jove!'

'What is it, dear?'

'Nothing. I just remembered a chap named Jones.'

However happily married, there are some things one never tells.

'Dash it all,' thought Major Wilbraham, 'I ought to have called at that place and got my money back.' And then, being a fair-minded man, he looked at the other side of the question. 'After all, it was I who broke the bargain. I suppose if I'd gone to see Jones something would have happened. And, anyway, as it turns out, if I hadn't been going to see Jones, I should never have heard Freda cry for help, and we might never have met. So, indirectly, perhaps they have a right to that fifty pounds!'

Mrs Wilbraham was also following out a train of thought. 'What a silly little fool I was to believe in that advertisement and pay those people three guineas. Of course, they never did anything for it and nothing ever happened. If I'd only known what was coming – first Mr Reid, and then the queer, romantic way that Charlie came into my life. And to think that *but for pure chance* I might never have met him!'

She turned and smiled adoringly at her husband.

The Red Signal

'No, but how too thrilling,' said pretty Mrs Eversleigh, opening her lovely, but slightly vacant eyes very wide. 'They always say women have a sixth sense; do you think it's true, Sir Alington?'

The famous alienist smiled sardonically. He had an unbounded contempt for the foolish pretty type, such as his fellow guest. Alington West was the supreme authority on mental disease, and he was fully alive to his own position and importance. A slightly pompous man of full figure.

'A great deal of nonsense is talked, I know that, Mrs Eversleigh. What does the term mean – a sixth sense?'

'You scientific men are always so severe. And it really is extraordinary the way one seems to positively know things sometimes – just know them, feel them, I mean – quite uncanny – it really is. Claire knows what I mean, don't you, Claire?'

She appealed to her hostess with a slight pout, and a tilted shoulder.

Claire Trent did not reply at once. It was a small dinner party, she and her husband, Violet Eversleigh, Sir Alington West, and his nephew, Dermot West, who was an old friend of Jack Trent's. Jack Trent himself, a somewhat heavy florid man, with a good-humoured smile, and a pleasant lazy laugh, took up the thread.

'Bunkum, Violet! Your best friend is killed in a railway

accident. Straight away you remember that you dreamt of a black cat last Tuesday – marvellous, you felt all along that something was going to happen!'

'Oh, no, Jack, you're mixing up premonitions with intuition now. Come, now, Sir Alington, you must admit that premonitions are real?'

'To a certain extent, perhaps,' admitted the physician cautiously. 'But coincidence accounts for a good deal, and then there is the invariable tendency to make the most of a story afterwards – you've always got to take that into account.'

'I don't think there is any such thing as premonition,' said Claire Trent, rather abruptly. 'Or intuition, or a sixth sense, or any of the things we talk about so glibly. We go through life like a train rushing through the darkness to an unknown destination.'

'That's hardly a good simile, Mrs Trent,' said Dermot West, lifting his head for the first time and taking part in the discussion. There was a curious glitter in the clear grey eyes that shone out rather oddly from the deeply tanned face. 'You've forgotten the signals, you see.'

'The signals?'

'Yes, green if its all right, and red – for danger!'

'Red – for danger – how thrilling!' breathed Violet Eversleigh.

Dermot turned from her rather impatiently.

'That's just a way of describing it, of course. Danger ahead! The red signal! Look out!'

Trent stared at him curiously.

'You speak as though it were an actual experience, Dermot, old boy.'

'So it is – has been, I mean.'

'Give us the yarn.'

'I can give you one instance. Out in Mesopotamia – just after the Armistice, I came into my tent one evening with the feeling strong upon me. Danger! Look out! Hadn't the ghost of a notion what it was all about. I made a round of the camp, fussed unnecessarily, took all precautions against an attack by hostile Arabs. Then I went back to my tent. As soon as I got inside, the feeling popped up again stronger than ever. Danger! In the end, I took a blanket outside, rolled myself up in it and slept there.'

'Well?'

'The next morning, when I went inside the tent, first thing I saw was a great knife arrangement – about half a yard long – struck down through my bunk, just where I would have lain. I soon found out about it – one of the Arab servants. His son had been shot as a spy. What have you got to say to that, Uncle Alington, as an example of what I call the red signal?'

The specialist smiled non-committally.

'A very interesting story, my dear Dermot.'

'But not one that you would accept unreservedly?'

'Yes, yes, I have no doubt that you had the premonition of danger, just as you state. But it is the origin of the premonition I dispute. According to you, it came from without, impressed by some outside source upon your mentality. But nowadays we find that nearly everything comes from within – from our subconscious self.'

'Good old subconscious,' cried Jack Trent. 'It's the jack-of-all-trades nowadays.'

Sir Alington continued without heeding the interruption.

'I suggest that by some glance or look this Arab had betrayed himself. Your conscious self did not notice or remember, but with your subconscious self it was otherwise. The subconscious never forgets. We believe, too, that it can reason and deduce quite independently of the higher or conscious will. Your subconscious self, then, believed that an attempt might be made to assassinate you, and succeeded in forcing its fear upon your conscious realization.'

'That sounds very convincing, I admit,' said Dermot, smiling.

'But not nearly so exciting,' pouted Mrs Eversleigh.

'It is also possible that you may have been subconsciously aware of the hate felt by the man towards you. What in the old days used to be called telepathy certainly exists, though the conditions governing it are very little understood.'

'Have there been any other instances?' asked Claire of Dermot.

'Oh! yes, but nothing very pictorial – and I suppose they could all be explained under the heading of coincidence. I refused an invitation to a country house once, for no other reason than the hoisting of the "red signal". The place was burnt out during the week. By the way, Uncle Alington, where does the subconscious come in there?'

'I'm afraid it doesn't,' said Alington, smiling.

'But you've got an equally good explanation. Come, now. No need to be tactful with near relatives.'

'Well, then, nephew, I venture to suggest that you refused the invitation for the ordinary reason that you didn't much want to go, and that after the fire, you suggested to yourself that you had had a warning of danger, which explanation you now believe implicitly.'

'It's hopeless,' laughed Dermot. 'It's heads you win, tails I lose.'

'Never mind, Mr West,' cried Violet Eversleigh. 'I believe in your Red Signal implicitly. Is the time in Mesopotamia the last time you had it?'

'Yes – until——'

'I beg your pardon?'

'Nothing.'

Dermot sat silent. The words which had nearly left his lips were: 'Yes, *until tonight*.' They had come quite unbidden to his lips, voicing a thought which had as yet not been consciously realized, but he was aware at once that they were true. The Red Signal was looming up out of the darkness. Danger! Danger at hand!

But why? What conceivable danger could there be here? Here in the house of his friends? At least – well, yes, there was that kind of danger. He looked at Claire Trent – her whiteness, her slenderness, the exquisite droop of her golden head. But that danger had been there for some time – it was never likely to get acute. For Jack Trent was his best friend, and more than his best friend, the man who had saved his life in Flanders and had been recommended for the VC for doing so. A good fellow, Jack, one of the best. Damned bad luck that he should have fallen in love with Jack's wife. He'd get over it some day, he supposed. A thing couldn't go on hurting like this for ever. One could starve it out – that was it, starve it out. It was not as though she would ever guess – and if she did guess, there was no danger of her caring. A statue, a beautiful statue, a thing of gold and ivory and pale pink coral . . . a toy for a king, not a real woman. . . .

Claire . . . the very thought of her name, uttered silently hurt him. . . . He must get over it. He'd cared for women before. . . . 'But not like this!' said something. 'Not like this.' Well, there it was. No danger there – heartache, yes, but not danger. Not the danger of the Red Signal. That was for something else.

He looked round the table and it struck him for the first time that it was rather an unusual little gathering. His uncle, for instance, seldom dined out in this small, informal way. It was not as though the Trents were old friends; until this evening Dermot had not been aware that he knew them at all.

To be sure, there was an excuse. A rather notorious medium was coming after dinner to give a *séance*. Sir Alington professed to be mildly interested in spiritualism. Yes, that was an excuse, certainly.

The word forced itself on his notice. An *excuse*. Was the *séance* just an excuse to make the specialist's presence at dinner natural? If so, what was the real object of his being here? A host of details came rushing into Dermot's mind, trifles unnoticed at the time, or, as his uncle would have said, unnoticed by the conscious mind.

The great physician had looked oddly, very oddly, at Claire more than once. He seemed to be watching her. She was uneasy under his scrutiny. She made little twitching motions with her hands. She was nervous, horribly nervous, and was it, could it be, *frightened*? Why was she frightened?

With a jerk, he came back to the conversation round the table. Mrs Eversleigh had got the great man talking upon his own subject.

'My dear lady,' he was saying, 'what *is* madness? I can assure you that the more we study the subject, the more difficult we find it to pronounce. We all practise a certain amount of self-deception, and when we carry it so far as to believe we are the Czar of Russia, we are shut up or restrained. But there is a long road before we reach that point. At what particular spot on it shall we erect a post and say "On this side sanity, on the other madness?" It can't be done, you know. And I will tell you this, if the man suffering from a delusion happened to hold his tongue about it, in all probability we should never be able to distinguish him from a normal individual. The extraordinary sanity of the insane is a most interesting subject.'

Sir Alington sipped his wine with appreciation, and beamed upon the company.

'I've always heard they are very cunning,' remarked Mrs Eversleigh. 'Loonies, I mean.'

'Remarkably so. And suppression of one's particular delusion has a disastrous effect very often. All suppressions are dangerous, as psychoanalysis has taught us. The man who has a harmless eccentricity, and can indulge it as such, seldom goes over the border line. But the man' – he paused – 'or woman who is to all appearances perfectly normal may be in reality a poignant source of danger to the community.'

His gaze travelled gently down the table to Claire, and then back again. He sipped his wine once more.

A horrible fear shook Dermot. Was *that* what he meant? Was *that* what he was driving at? Impossible, but——

'And all from suppressing oneself,' sighed Mrs Eversleigh. 'I quite see that one should be very careful always to – to express one's personality. The dangers of the other are frightful.'

'My dear Mrs Eversleigh,' expostulated the physician. 'You have quite misunderstood me. The cause of the mischief is in the physical matter of the brain – sometimes arising from some outward agency such as a blow; sometimes, alas, congenital.'

'Heredity is so sad,' sighed the lady vaguely. 'Consumption and all that.'

'Tuberculosis is not hereditary,' said Sir Alington drily.

'Isn't it? I always thought it was. But madness is! How dreadful. What else?'

'Gout,' said Sir Alington, smiling. 'And colour blindness – the latter is rather interesting. It is transmitted direct to males, but is latent in females. So, while there are many colourblind men, for a woman to be colourblind, it must have been latent in her mother as well as present in her father – rather an unusual state of things to occur. That is what is called sex-limited heredity.'

'How interesting. But madness is not like that, is it?'

'Madness can be handed down to men or women equally,' said the physician gravely.

Claire rose suddenly, pushing back her chair so abruptly that it overturned and fell to the ground. She was very pale and the nervous motions of her fingers were very apparent.

'You – you will not be long, will you?' she begged. 'Mrs Thompson will be here in a few minutes now.'

'One glass of port, and I will be with you, for one,' declared Sir Alington. 'To see this wonderful Mrs Thompson's performance is what I have come for, is it not? Ha, ha! Not that I needed any inducement.' He bowed.

Claire gave a faint smile of acknowledgment and passed out of the room, her hand on Mrs Eversleigh's shoulder.

'Afraid I've been talking shop,' remarked the physician as he resumed his seat. 'Forgive me, my dear fellow.'

'Not at all,' said Trent perfunctorily.

He looked strained and worried. For the first time Dermot felt an outsider in the company of his friend. Between these two was a secret that even an old friend might not share. And yet the whole thing was fantastic and incredible. What had he to go upon? Nothing but a couple of glances and a woman's nervousness.

They lingered over their wine but a very short time, and arrived up in the drawing-room just as Mrs Thompson was announced.

The medium was a plump middle-aged woman, atrociously dressed in magenta velvet, with a loud rather common voice.

'Hope I'm not late, Mrs Trent,' she said cheerily. 'You did say nine o'clock, didn't you?'

'You are quite punctual, Mrs Thompson,' said Claire in her sweet, slight husky voice. 'This is our little circle.'

No further introductions were made, as was evidently the custom. The medium swept them all with a shrewd, penetrating eye.

'I hope we shall get some good results,' she remarked briskly. 'I can't tell you how I hate it when I go out and I can't give satisfaction, so to speak. It just makes me mad. But I think Shiromako (my Japanese control, you know) will be able to get through all right tonight. I'm feeling ever so fit, and I refused the welsh rabbit, fond of toasted cheese though I am.'

Dermot listened, half amused, half disgusted. How prosaic the whole thing was! And yet, was he not judging foolishly? Everything, after all, was natural – the powers claimed by mediums were natural powers, as yet imperfectly understood. A great surgeon might be wary of indigestion on the eve of a delicate operation. Why not Mrs Thompson?

Chairs were arranged in a circle, lights so that they could

conveniently be raised or lowered. Dermot noticed that there was no question of *tests*, or of Sir Alington satisfying himself as to the conditions of the *séance*. No, this business of Mrs Thompson was only a blind. Sir Alington was here for quite another purpose. Claire's mother, Dermot remembered, had died abroad. There had been some mystery about her. . . . Hereditary. . . .

With a jerk he forced his mind back to the surroundings of the moment.

Everyone took their places, and the lights were turned out, all but a small red-shaded one on a far table.

For a while nothing was heard but the low even breathing of the medium. Gradually it grew more and more stertorous. Then, with a suddenness that made Dermot jump, a loud rap came from the far end of the room. It was repeated from the other side. Then a perfect crescendo of raps was heard. They died away, and a sudden high peal of mocking laughter rang through the room. Then silence, broken by a voice utterly unlike that of Mrs Thompson, a high-pitched quaintly inflected voice.

'I am here, gentlemen,' it said. 'Yess, I am here. You wish ask me things?'

'Who are you? Shiromako?'

'Yess. I Shiromako. I pass over long time ago. I work. I very happy.'

Further details of Shiromako's life followed. It was all very flat and uninteresting, and Dermot had heard it often before. Everyone was happy, very happy. Messages were given from vaguely described relatives, the description being so loosely worded as to fit almost any contingency. An elderly lady, the mother of someone present, held the floor for some time, imparting copy book maxims with an air of refreshing novelty hardly borne out by her subject matter.

'Someone else want to get through now,' announced Shiromako. 'Got a very important message for one of the gentlemen.'

There was a pause, and then a new voice spoke, prefacing its remark with an evil demoniacal chuckle.

'Ha, ha! Ha, ha, ha! Better not go home. Better not go home. Take my advice.'

'Who are you speaking to?' asked Trent.

'One of you three. I shouldn't go home if I were him. Danger! Blood! Not very much blood – quite enough. No, don't go home.' The voice grew fainter. '*Don't go home!*'

It died away completely. Dermot felt his blood tingling. He was convinced that the warning was meant for him. Somehow or other, there was danger abroad tonight.

There was a sigh from the medium, and then a groan. She was coming round. The lights were turned on, and presently she sat upright, her eyes blinking a little.

'Go off well, my dear? I hope so.'

'Very good indeed, thank you, Mrs Thompson.'

'Shiromako, I suppose?'

'Yes, and others.'

Mrs Thompson yawned.

'I'm dead beat. Absolutely down and out. Does fairly take it out of you. Well, I'm glad it was a success. I was a bit afraid it mightn't be – afraid something disagreeable might happen. There's a queer feel about this room tonight.'

She glanced over each ample shoulder in turn, and then shrugged them uncomfortably.

'I don't like it,' she said. 'Any sudden deaths among any of you people lately?'

'What do you mean – among us?'

'Near relatives – dear friends? No? Well, if I wanted to be melodramatic, I'd say there was death in the air tonight. There, it's only my nonsense. Goodbye, Mrs Trent. I'm glad you've been satisfied.'

Mrs Thompson in her magenta velvet gown went out.

'I hope you've been interested, Sir Alington,' murmured Claire.

'A most interesting evening, my dear lady. Many thanks

for the opportunity. Let me wish you good night. You are all going to a dance, are you not?'

'Won't you come with us?'

'No, no. I make it a rule to be in bed by half past eleven. Good night. Good night, Mrs Eversleigh. Ah! Dermot, I rather want to have a word with you. Can you come with me now? You can rejoin the others at the Grafton Galleries.'

'Certainly, uncle. I'll meet you there then, Trent.'

Very few words were exchanged between uncle and nephew during the short drive to Harley Street, Sir Alington made a semi-apology for dragging Dermot away, and assured him that he would only detain him a few minutes.

'Shall I keep the car for you, my boy?' he asked, as they alighted.

'Oh, don't bother, uncle. I'll pick up a taxi.'

'Very good. I don't like to keep Charlson up later than I can help. Good night, Charlson. Now where the devil did I put my key?'

The car glided away as Sir Alington stood on the steps vainly searching his pockets.

'Must have left it in my other coat,' he said at length. 'Ring the bell, will you? Johnson is still up. I dare say.'

The imperturbable Johnson did indeed open the door within sixty seconds.

'Mislaid my key, Johnson,' explained Sir Alington. 'Bring a couple of whiskies and sodas into the library, will you?'

'Very good, Sir Alington.'

The physician strode on into the library and turned on the lights. He motioned to Dermot to close the door behind him after entering.

'I won't keep you long, Dermot, but there's just something I want to say to you. Is it my fancy, or have you a certain – *tendresse*, shall we say, for Mrs Jack Trent?'

The blood rushed to Dermot's face.

'Jack Trent is my best friend.'

'Pardon me, but that is hardly answering my question. I dare say that you consider my views on divorce and such matters highly puritanical, but I must remind you that you are my only near relative and that you are my heir.'

'There is no question of a divorce,' said Dermot angrily.

'There certainly is not, for a reason which I understand perhaps better than you do. That particular reason I cannot give you now, but I do wish to warn you. Claire Trent is not for you.'

The young man faced his uncle's gaze steadily.

'I do understand – and permit me to say, perhaps better than you think. I know the reason for your presence at dinner tonight.'

'Eh?' The physician was clearly startled. 'How did you know that?'

'Call it a guess, sir. I am right, am I not, when I say that you were there in your – professional capacity.'

Sir Alington strode up and down.

'You are quite right, Dermot. I could not, of course, have told you so myself, though I am afraid it will soon be common property.'

Dermot's heart contracted.

'You mean that you have – made up your mind?'

'Yes, there is insanity in the family – on the mother's side. A sad case – a very sad case.'

'I can't believe it, sir.'

'I dare say not. To the layman there are few if any signs apparent.'

'And to the expert?'

'The evidence is conclusive. In such a case, the patient must be placed under restraint as soon as possible.'

'My God!' breathed Dermot. 'But you can't shut anyone up for nothing at all.'

'My dear Dermot! Cases are only placed under restraint when their being at large would result in danger to the community.

'Very grave danger. In all probability a peculiar form of homicidal mania. It was so in the mother's case.'

Dermot turned away with a groan, burying his face in his hands. Claire – white and golden Claire!

'In the circumstances,' continued the physician comfortably, 'I felt it incumbent on me to warn you.'

'Claire,' murmured Dermot. 'My poor Claire.'

'Yes, indeed, we must all pity her.'

Suddenly Dermot raised his head.

'I don't believe it.'

'What?'

'I say I don't believe it. Doctors make mistakes. Every one knows that. And they're always keen on their own speciality.'

'My dear Dermot,' cried Sir Alington angrily.

'I tell you I don't believe it – and anyway, even if it is so, I don't care. I love Claire. If she will come with me, I shall take her away – far away – out of the reach of meddling physicians. I shall guard her, care for her, shelter her with my love.'

'You will do nothing of the sort. Are you mad?'

Dermot laughed scornfully.

'*You* would say so, I dare say.'

'Understand me, Dermot.' Sir Alington's face was red with suppressed passion. 'If you do this this – this shameful thing – it is the end. I shall withdraw the allowance I am now making you, and I shall make a new will leaving all I possess to various hospitals.'

'Do as you please with your damned money,' said Dermot in a low voice. 'I shall have the woman I love.'

'A woman who——'

'Say a word against her, and, by God! I'll kill you!' cried Dermot.

A slight clink of glasses made them both swing round. Unheard by them in the heat of their argument, Johnson had entered with a tray of glasses. His face was the imperturbable one of the good servant, but Dermot wondered how much he had overheard.

'That'll do, Johnson,' said Sir Alington curtly. 'You can go to bed.'

'Thank you, sir. Good night, sir.'

Johnson withdrew.

The two men looked at each other. The momentary interruption had calmed the storm.

'Uncle,' said Dermot. 'I shouldn't have spoken to you as I did. I can quite see that from your point of view you are perfectly right. But I have loved Claire Trent for a long time. The fact that Jack Trent is my best friend has hitherto stood in the way of my ever speaking of love to Claire herself. But in these circumstances that fact no longer counts. The idea that any monetary conditions can deter me is absurd. I think we've both said all there is to be said. Good night.'

'Dermot——'

'It is really no good arguing further. Good night, Uncle Alington. I'm sorry, but there it is.'

He went out quickly, shutting the door behind him. The hall was in darkness. He passed through it, opened the front door and emerged into the street, banging the door behind him.

A taxi had just deposited a fare at a house farther along the street and Dermot hailed it, and drove to the Grafton Galleries.

In the door of the ballroom he stood for a minute bewildered, his head spinning. The raucous jazz music, the smiling women – it was as though he had stepped into another world.

Had he dreamt it all? Impossible that that grim conversation with his uncle should have really taken place. There was Claire floating past, like a lily in her white and silver gown that fitted sheathlike to her slenderness. She smiled at him, her face calm and serene. Surely it was all a dream.

The dance had stopped. Presently she was near him, smiling up into his face. As in a dream he asked her to dance.

She was in his arms now, the raucous melodies had begun again.

He felt her flag a little.

'Tired? Do you want to stop?'

'If you don't mind. Can we go somewhere where we can talk. There is something I want to say to you.'

Not a dream. He came back to earth with a bump. Could he ever have thought her face calm and serene? It was haunted with anxiety, with dread. How much did she know?

He found a quiet corner, and they sat down side by side.

'Well,' he said, assuming a lightness he did not feel. 'You said you had something you wanted to say to me?'

'Yes.' Her eyes were cast down. She was playing nervously with the tassel of her gown. 'It's difficult – rather.'

'Tell me, Claire.'

'It's just this. I want you to – to go away for a time.'

He was astonished. Whatever he had expected, it was not this.

'You want me to go away? Why?'

'It's best to be honest, isn't it? I – I know that you are a – a gentleman and my friend. I want you to go away because I – I have let myself get fond of you.'

'Claire.'

Her words left him dumb – tongue-tied.

'Please do not think that I am conceited enough to fancy that you – that you would ever be likely to fall in love with me. It is only that – that I am not very happy – and – oh! I would rather you went away.'

'Claire, don't you know that I have cared – cared damnably – ever since I met you?'

She lifted startled eyes to his face.

'You cared? You have cared a long time?'

'Since the beginning.'

'Oh!' she cried. 'Why didn't you tell me? Then? When I could have come to you! Why tell me now when it's too late.

No, I'm mad – I don't know what I'm saying. I could never have come to you.'

'Claire, what did you mean when you said "now that it's too late?" Is it – is it because of my uncle? What he knows? What he thinks?'

She nodded dumbly, the tears running down her face.

'Listen, Claire, you're not to believe all that. You're not to think about it. Instead you will come away with me. We'll go to the South Seas, to islands like green jewels. You will be happy there, and I will look after you – keep you safe for always.'

His arms went round her. He drew her to him, felt her tremble at his touch. Then suddenly she wrenched herself free.

'Oh, no, please. Can't you see? I couldn't now. It would be ugly – ugly – ugly. All along I've wanted to be good – and now – it would be ugly as well.'

He hesitated, baffled by her words. She looked at him appealingly.

'Please,' she said. 'I want to be good . . .'

Without a word, Dermot got up and left her. For the moment he was touched and racked by her words beyond argument. He went for his hat and coat, running into Trent as he did so.

'Hallo, Dermot, you're off early.'

'Yes, I'm not in the mood for dancing tonight.'

'It's a rotten night,' said Trent gloomily. 'But you haven't got my worries.'

Dermot had a sudden panic that Trent might be going to confide in him. Not that – anything but that!

'Well, so long,' he said hurriedly. 'I'm off home.'

'Home, eh? What about the warning of the spirits?'

'I'll risk that. Good night, Jack.'

Dermot's flat was not far away. He walked there, feeling the need of the cool night air to calm his fevered brain.

He let himself in with his key and switched on the light in his bedroom.

And all at once, for the second time that night, the feeling that he had designated by the title of the Red Signal surged over him. So overpowering was it that for the moment it swept even Claire from his mind.

Danger! He was in danger. At this very moment, in this very room, he was in danger.

He tried in vain to ridicule himself free of the fear. Perhaps his efforts were secretly half hearted. So far, the Red Signal had given him timely warning which had enabled him to avoid disaster. Smiling a little at his own superstition, he made a careful tour of the flat. It was possible that some malefactor had got in and was lying concealed there. But his search revealed nothing. His man, Milson, was away, and the flat was absolutely empty.

He returned to his bedroom and undressed slowly, frowning to himself. The sense of danger was acute as ever. He went to a drawer to get out a handkerchief, and suddenly stood stock still. There was an unfamiliar lump in the middle of the drawer – something hard.

His quick nervous fingers tore aside the handkerchiefs and took out the object concealed beneath them. It was a revolver.

With the utmost astonishment Dermot examined it keenly. It was of a somewhat unfamiliar pattern, and one shot had been fired from it lately. Beyond that, he could make nothing of it. Someone had placed it in that drawer that very evening. It had not been there when he dressed for dinner – he was sure of that.

He was about to replace it in the drawer, when he was startled by a bell ringing. It rang again and again, sounding unusually loud in the quietness of the empty flat.

Who could it be coming to the front door at this hour? And only one answer came to the question – an answer instinctive and persistent.

'Danger – danger – danger. . . .'

Led by some instinct for which he did not account. Dermot switched off his light, slipped on an overcoat that lay across a chair, and opened the hall door.

Two men stood outside. Beyond them Dermot caught sight of a blue uniform. A policeman!

'Mr West?' asked the foremost of the two men.

It seemed to Dermot that ages elapsed before he answered. In reality it was only a few seconds before he replied in a very fair imitation of his man's expressionless voice:

'Mr West hasn't come in yet. What do you want with him at this time of night?'

'Hasn't come in yet, eh? Very well, then, I think we'd better come in and wait for him.'

'No, you don't.'

'See here, my man, my name is Inspector Verall of Scotland Yard, and I've got a warrant for the arrest of your master. You can see it if you like.'

Dermot perused the proffered paper, or pretended to do so, asking in a dazed voice:

'What for? What's he done?'

'Murder. Sir Alington West of Harley Street.'

His brain in a whirl, Dermot fell back before his redoubtable visitors. He went into the sitting-room and switched on the light. The inspector followed him.

'Have a search round,' he directed the other man. Then he turned to Dermot.

'You stay here, my man. No slipping off to warn your master. What's you name, by the way?'

'Milson, sir.'

'What time do you expect your master in, Milson?'

'I don't know, sir, he was going to a dance, I believe. At the Grafton Galleries.'

'He left there just under an hour ago. Sure he's not been back here?'

'I don't think so, sir. I fancy I should have heard him come in.'

At this moment the second man came in from the adjoining room. In his hand he carried the revolver. He took it across to the inspector in some excitement. An expression of satisfaction flitted across the latter's face.

'That settles it,' he remarked. 'Must have slipped in and out without your hearing him. He's hooked it by now. I'd better be off. Cawley, you stay here, in case he should come back again, and you can keep an eye on this fellow. He may know more about his master than he pretends.'

The inspector bustled off. Dermot endeavoured to get at the details of the affair from Cawley, who was quite ready to be talkative.

'Pretty clear case,' he vouchsafed. 'The murder was discovered almost immediately. Johnson, the manservant, had only just gone up to bed when he fancied he heard a shot, and came down again. Found Sir Alington dead, shot through the heart. He rang us up at once and we came along and heard his story.'

'Which made it a pretty clear case?' ventured Dermot.

'Absolutely. This young West came in with his uncle and they were quarrelling when Johnson brought in the drinks. The old boy was threatening to make a new will, and your master was talking about shooting him. Not five minutes later the shot was heard. Oh! yes, clear enough. Silly young fool!'

Clear enough indeed. Dermot's heart sank as he realized the overwhelming nature of the evidence against him. Danger indeed – horrible danger! And no way out save that of flight. He set his wits to work. Presently he suggested making a cup of tea. Cawley assented readily enough. He had already searched the flat and knew there was no back entrance.

Dermot was permitted to depart to the kitchen. Once there he put the kettle on, and chinked cups and saucers industriously. Then he stole swiftly to the window and lifted the sash. The flat was on the second floor, and outside the window was a small wire lift used by tradesmen which ran up and down on its steel cable.

Like a flash Dermot was outside the window and swinging himself down the wire rope. It cut into his hands, making them bleed, but he went on desperately.

A few minutes later he was emerging cautiously from the back of the block. Turning the corner, he cannoned into a figure standing by the sidewalk. To his utter amazement he recognized Jack Trent. Trent was fully alive to the perils of the situation.

'My God! Dermot! Quick, don't hang about here.'

Taking him by the arm, he led him down a by-street, then down another. A lonely taxi was sighted and hailed and they jumped in, Trent giving the man his own address.

'Safest place for the moment. There we can decide what to do next to put those fools off the track. I came round here hoping to be able to warn you before the police got here, but I was too late.'

'I didn't even know that you had heard of it. Jack, you don't believe——'

'Of course not, old fellow, not for one minute. I know you far too well. All the same, it's a nasty business for you. They came round asking questions – what time you got to the Grafton Galleries, when you left, etc. Dermot, who could have done the old boy in?'

'I can't imagine. Whoever did it put the revolver in my drawer, I suppose. Must have been watching us pretty closely.'

'That *séance* business was damned funny. '*Don't go home.*' Meant for poor old West. He did go home, and got shot.'

'It applies to me too,' said Dermot. 'I went home and found a planted revolver and a police inspector.'

'Well, I hope it doesn't get me too,' said Trent. 'Here we are.'

He paid the taxi, opened the door with his latch-key, and

guided Dermot up the dark stairs to his den, which was a small room on the first floor.

He threw open the door and Dermot walked in, whilst Trent switched on the light, and then came to join him.

'Pretty safe here for the time being,' he remarked. 'Now we can get our heads together and decide what is best to be done.'

'I've made a fool of myself,' said Dermot suddenly. 'I ought to have faced it out. I see more clearly now. The whole thing's a plot. What the devil are you laughing at?'

For Trent was leaning back in his chair, shaking with unrestrained mirth. There was something horrible in the sound – something horrible, too, about the man altogether. There was a curious light in his eyes.

'A damned clever plot,' he gasped out. 'Dermot, my boy, you're done for.'

He drew the telephone towards him.

'What are you going to do?' asked Dermot.

'Ring up Scotland Yard. Tell 'em their bird's here – safe under lock and key. Yes, I locked the door when I came in and the key's in my pocket. No good looking at that other door behind me. That leads into Claire's room, and she always locks it on her side. She's afraid of me, you know. Been afraid of me a long time. She always knows when I'm thinking about that knife – a long sharp knife. No, you don't——'

Dermot had been about to make a rush at him, but the other had suddenly produced an ugly-looking revolver.

'That's the second of them,' chuckled Trent. 'I put the first of them in your drawer – after shooting old West with it—— What are you looking at over my head? That door? It's no use, even if Claire was to open it – and she might to *you* – I'd shoot you before you got there. Not in the heart – not to kill, just wing you, so that you couldn't get away. I'm a jolly good shot, you know. I saved your life once. More fool I. No, no, I want you hanged – yes, hanged. It isn't you I want the knife for. It's Claire – pretty Claire, so white and soft. Old West knew. That's what he was here for tonight, to see if I was mad or not. He wanted to shut me up – so that I shouldn't get at Claire with the knife. I was very cunning. I took his latchkey and yours too. I slipped away from the dance as soon as I got there. I saw you come out from his house, and I went in. I shot him and came away at once. Then I went to your place and left the revolver. I was at the Grafton Galleries again almost as soon as you were, and I put the latchkey back in your coat pocket when I was saying good night to you. I don't mind telling you all this. There's no one else to hear, and when you're being hanged I'd like you to know I did it. . . . God, how it makes me laugh! What are you thinking of? What the devil are you looking at?'

'I'm thinking of some words you quoted just now. You'd have done better, Trent, not to come home.'

'What do you mean?'

'Look behind you?'

Trent spun round. In the doorway of the communicating room stood Claire – and Inspector Verall. . . .

Trent was quick. The revolver spoke just once – and found its mark. He fell forward across the table. The inspector sprang to his side, as Dermot stared at Claire in a dream. Thoughts flashed through his brain disjointedly. His uncle – their quarrel – the colossal misunderstanding – the divorce laws of England which would never free Claire from an insane husband – 'we must all pity her' – the plot between her and Sir Alington which the cunning of Trent had seen through – her cry to him, 'Ugly – ugly – ugly!' Yes, but now——

The inspector straightened up again.

'Dead,' he said vexedly.

'Yes.' Dermot heard himself saying, 'he was always a good shot. . . .'

The Girl in the Train

'And that's that!' observed George Rowland ruefully, as he gazed up at the imposing smoke-grimed façade of the building he had just quitted.

It might be said to represent very aptly the power of Money – and Money, in the person of William Rowland, uncle to the aforementioned George, had just spoken its mind very freely. In the course of a brief ten minutes, from being the apple of his uncle's eye, the heir to his wealth, and a young man with a promising business career in front of him, George had suddenly become one of the vast army of the unemployed.

'And in these clothes they won't even give me the dole,' reflected Mr Rowland gloomily, 'and as for writing poems and selling them at the door at twopence (or "what you care to give, lydy") I simply haven't got the brains.'

It was true that George embodied a veritable triumph of the tailor's art. He was exquisitely and beautifully arrayed. Solomon and the lilies of the field were simply not in it with George. But man cannot live by clothes alone – unless he has had some considerable training in the art – and Mr Rowland was painfully aware of the fact.

'And all because of that rotten show last night,' he reflected sadly.

The rotten show last night had been a Covent Garden Ball. Mr Rowland had returned from it at a somewhat late – or rather early – hour – as a matter of fact, he could not strictly say that he remembered returning at all. Rogers, his uncle's butler, was a helpful fellow, and could doubtless give more details on the matter. A splitting head, a cup of strong tea, and an arrival at the office at five minutes to twelve instead of half-past nine had precipitated the catastrophe. Mr Rowland, senior, who for twenty-four years had condoned and paid up as a tactful relative should, had suddenly abandoned these tactics and revealed himself in a totally new light. The inconsequence of George's replies (the young man's head was still opening and shutting like some mediæval instrument of the Inquisition) had displeased him still further. William Rowland was nothing if not thorough. He cast his nephew adrift upon the world in a few short succinct words, and then settled down to his interrupted survey of some oilfields in Peru.

George Rowland shook the dust of his uncle's office from off his feet, and stepped out into the City of London. George was a practical fellow. A good lunch, he considered, was essential to a review of the situation. He had it. Then he retraced his steps to the family mansion. Rogers opened the door. His well-trained face expressed no surprise at seeing George at this unusual hour.

'Good afternoon, Rogers. Just pack up my things for me, will you? I'm leaving here.'

'Yes, sir. Just for a short visit, sir?'

'For good, Rogers. I am going to the colonies this afternoon.'

'Indeed, sir?'

'Yes. That is, if there is a suitable boat. Do you know anything about the boats, Rogers?'

'Which colony were you thinking of visiting, sir?'

'I'm not particular. Any of 'em will do. Let's say Australia. What do you think of the idea, Rogers?'

Rogers coughed discreetly.

'Well, sir, I've certainly heard it said that there's room out there for any one who really wants to work.'

Mr Rowland gazed at him with interest and admiration.

'Very neatly put, Rogers. Just what I was thinking myself. I shan't go to Australia – not today, at any rate. Fetch me an *ABC*, will you? We will select something nearer at hand.'

Rogers brought the required volume. George opened it at random and turned the pages with a rapid hand.

'Perth – too far away – Putney Bridge – too near at hand. Ramsgate? I think not. Reigate also leaves me cold. Why – what an extraordinary thing! There's actually a place called Rowland's Castle. Ever heard of it, Rogers?'

'I fancy, sir, that you go there from Waterloo.'

'What an extraordinary fellow you are, Rogers. You know everything. Well, well, Rowland's Castle! I wonder what sort of a place it is.'

'Not much of a place, I should say, sir.'

'All the better; there'll be less competition. These quiet little country hamlets have a lot of the old feudal spirit knocking about. The last of the original Rowlands ought to meet with instant appreciation. I shouldn't wonder if they elected me mayor in a week.'

He shut up the *ABC* with a bang.

'The die is cast. Pack me a small suit-case, will you, Rogers? Also my compliments to the cook, and will she oblige me with a loan of the cat. Dick Whittington, you know. When you set out to become a Lord Mayor, a cat is essential.'

'I'm sorry, sir, but the cat is not available at the present moment.'

'How is that?'

'A family of eight, sir. Arrived this morning.'

'You don't say so. I thought its name was Peter.'

'So it is, sir. A great surprise to all of us.'

'A case of careless christening and the deceitful sex, eh? Well, well, I shall have to go catless. Pack up those things at once, will you?'

'Very good, sir.'

Rogers withdrew, to reappear ten minutes later.

'Shall I call a taxi, sir?'

'Yes, please.'

Rogers hesitated, then advanced a little farther into the room.

'You'll excuse the liberty, sir, but if I was you, I shouldn't take too much notice of anything Mr Rowland said this morning. He was at one of those city dinners last night, and——'

'Say no more,' said George. 'I understand.'

'And being inclined to gout——'

'I know, I know. Rather a strenuous evening for you, Rogers, with two of us, eh? But I've set my heart on distinguishing myself at Rowland's Castle – the cradle of my historic race – that would go well in a speech, wouldn't it? A wire to me there, or a discreet advertisement in the morning papers, will recall me at any time if a fricassée of veal is in preparation. And now – to Waterloo! – as Wellington said on the eve of the historic battle.'

Waterloo Station was not at its brightest and best that afternoon. Mr Rowland eventually discovered a train that would take him to his destination, but it was an undistinguished train, an unimposing train – a train that nobody seemed anxious to travel by. Mr Rowland had a first-class carriage to himself, up in the front of the train. A fog was descending in an indeterminate way over the metropolis, now it lifted, now it descended. The platform was deserted, and only the asthmatic breathing of the engine broke the silence.

And then, all of a sudden, things began to happen with bewildering rapidity.

A girl happened first. She wrenched open the door and

jumped in, rousing Mr Rowland from something perilously near a nap, exclaiming as she did so: 'Oh! hide me – oh! please hide me.'

George was essentially a man of action – his not to reason why, his but to do and die, etc. There is only one place to hide in a railway carriage – under the seat. In seven seconds the girl was bestowed there, and George's suit-case, negligently standing on end, covered her retreat. None too soon. An infuriated face appeared at the carriage window.

'My niece! You have her here. I want my niece.'

George, a little breathless, was reclining in the corner, deep in the sporting column of the evening paper, one-thirty edition. He laid it aside with the air of a man recalling himself from far away.

'I beg your pardon, sir?' he said politely.

'My niece – what have you done with her?'

Acting on the policy that attack is always better than defence, George leaped into action.

'What the devil do you mean?' he cried, with a very creditable imitation of his own uncle's manner.

The other paused a minute, taken aback by this sudden fierceness. He was a fat man, still panting a little as though he had run some way. His hair was cut *en brosse*, and he had a moustache of the Hohenzollern persuasion. His accents were decidedly guttural, and the stiffness of his carriage denoted that he was more at home in uniform than out of it. George had the true-born Briton's prejudice against foreigners – and an especial distaste for German-looking foreigners.

'What the devil do you mean, sir?' he repeated angrily.

'She came in here,' said the other. 'I saw her. What have you done with her?'

George flung aside the paper and thrust his head and shoulders through the window.

'So that's it, is it?' he roared. 'Blackmail. But you've tried it on the wrong person. I read all about you in the *Daily Mail* this morning. Here, guard, guard!'

Already attracted from afar by the altercation, that functionary came hurrying up.

'Here, guard,' said Mr Rowland, with that air of authority which the lower classes so adore. 'This fellow is annoying me. I'll give him in charge for attempted blackmail if necessary. Pretends I've got his niece hidden here. There's a regular gang of these foreigners trying this sort of thing on. It ought to be stopped. Take him away, will you? Here's my card if you want it.'

The guard looked from one to the other. His mind was soon made up. His training led him to despise foreigners, and to respect and admire well-dressed gentlemen who travelled first class.

He laid his hand on the shoulder of the intruder.

'Here,' he said, 'you come out of this.'

At this crisis the stranger's English failed him, and he plunged into passionate profanity in his native tongue.

'That's enough of that,' said the guard. 'Stand away, will you? She's due out.'

Flags were waved and whistles were blown. With an unwilling jerk the train drew out of the station.

George remained at his observation post until they were clear of the platform. Then he drew in his head, and picking up the suit-case tossed it into the rack.

'It's quite all right. You can come out,' he said reassuringly.

The girl crawled out.

'Oh!' she gasped. 'How can I thank you?'

'That's quite all right. It's been a pleasure, I assure you,' returned George nonchalantly.

He smiled at her reassuringly. There was a slightly puzzled look in her eyes. She seemed to be missing something to which she was accustomed. At that moment, she caught sight of herself in the narrow glass opposite, and gave a heartfelt gasp.

Whether the carriage cleaners do, or do not, sweep under

the seats every day is doubtful. Appearances were against their doing so, but it may be that every particle of dirt and smoke finds its way there like a homing bird. George had hardly had time to take in the girl's appearance, so sudden had been her arrival, and so brief the space of time before she crawled into hiding, but it was certainly a trim and well-dressed young woman who had disappeared under the seat. Now her little red hat was crushed and dented, and her face was disfigured with long streaks of dirt.

'Oh!' said the girl.

She fumbled for her bag. George, with the tact of a true gentleman, looked fixedly out of the window and admired the streets of London south of the Thames.

'How can I thank you?' said the girl again.

Taking this as a hint that conversation might now be resumed, George withdrew his gaze, and made another polite disclaimer, but this time with a good deal of added warmth in his manner.

The girl was absolutely lovely! Never before, George told himself, had he seen such a lovely girl. The *empressement* of his manner became even more marked.

'I think it was simply splendid of you,' said the girl with enthusiasm.

'Not at all. Easiest thing in the world. Only too pleased been of use,' mumbled George.

'Splendid,' she reiterated emphatically.

It is undoubtedly pleasant to have the loveliest girl you have ever seen gazing into your eyes and telling you how splendid you are. George enjoyed it as much as any one would.

Then there came a rather difficult silence. It seemed to dawn upon the girl that further explanations might be expected. She flushed a little.

'The awkward part of it is,' she said nervously, 'that I'm afraid I can't explain.'

She looked at him with a piteous air of uncertainty.

'You can't explain?'

'No.'

'How perfectly splendid!' said Mr Rowland with enthusiasm.'

'I beg your pardon?'

'I said, How perfectly splendid. Just like one of those books that keep you up all night. The heroine always says "I can't explain" in the first chapter. She explains in the last, of course, and there's never any real reason why she shouldn't have done so in the beginning – except that it would spoil the story. I can't tell you how pleased I am to be mixed up in a real mystery – I didn't know there were such things. I hope it's got something to do with secret documents of immense importance, and the Balkan express. I dote upon the Balkan express.'

The girl stared at him with wide, suspicious eyes.

'What makes you say the Balkan express?' she asked sharply.

'I hope I haven't been indiscreet,' George hastened to put in. 'Your uncle travelled by it, perhaps.'

'My uncle——' She paused, then began again. 'My uncle——'

'Quite so,' said George sympathetically. 'I've got an uncle myself. Nobody should be held responsible for their uncles. Nature's little throw-backs – that's how I look at it.'

The girl began to laugh suddenly. When she spoke George was aware of the slight foreign inflection in her voice. At first he had taken her to be English.

'What a refreshing and unusual person you are, Mr——'

'Rowland. George to my friends.'

'My name is Elizabeth——'

She stopped abruptly.

'I like the name of Elizabeth,' said George, to cover her momentary confusion. 'They don't call you Bessie, or anything horrible like that, I hope?'

She shook her head.

'Well,' said George, 'now that we know each other, we'd

better get down to business. If you'll stand up, Elizabeth, I'll brush down the back of your coat.'

She stood up obediently, and George was as good as his word.

'Thank you, Mr Rowland.'

'George. George to my friends, remember. And you can't come into my nice empty carriage, roll under the seat, induce me to tell lies to your uncle, and then refuse to be friends, can you?'

'Thank you, George.'

'That's better.'

'Do I look quite all right now?' asked Elizabeth, trying to see over her left shoulder.

'You look – oh! you look – you look all right,' said George, curbing himself sternly.

'It was all so sudden, you see,' explained the girl.

'It must have been.'

'He saw us in the taxi, and then at the station I just bolted in here knowing he was close behind me. Where is this train going to, by the way?'

'Rowland's Castle,' said George firmly.

The girl looked puzzled.

'Rowland's Castle?'

'Not at once, of course. Only after a good deal of stopping and slow going. But I confidently expect to be there before midnight. The old South-Western was a very reliable line – slow but sure – and I'm sure the Southern Railway is keeping up the old traditions.'

'I don't know that I want to go to Rowland's Castle,' said Elizabeth doubtfully.

'You hurt me. It's a delightful spot.'

'Have you ever been there?'

'Not exactly. But there are lots of other places you can go to, if you don't fancy Rowland's Castle. There's Woking, and Weybridge, and Wimbledon. The train is sure to stop at one or other of them.'

'I see,' said the girl. 'Yes, I can get out there, and perhaps motor back to London. That would be the best plan, I think.'

Even as she spoke, the train began to slow up. Mr Rowland gazed at her with appealing eyes.

'If I can do anything——'

'No, indeed. You've done a lot already.'

There was a pause, then the girl broke out suddenly:

'I – I wish I could explain. I——'

'For heaven's sake don't do that! It would spoil everything. But look here, isn't there anything that I could do? Carry the secret papers to Vienna – or something of that kind? There always are secret papers. Do give me a chance.'

The train had stopped. Elizabeth jumped quickly out on to the platform. She turned and spoke to him through the window.

'Are you in earnest? Would you really do something for us – for me?'

'I'd do anything in the world for you, Elizabeth.'

'Even if I could give you no reasons?'

'Rotten things, reasons!'

'Even if it were – dangerous?'

'The more danger, the better.'

She hesitated a minute then seemed to make up her mind.

'Lean out of the window. Look down the platform as though you weren't really looking.' Mr Rowland endeavoured to comply with this somewhat difficult recommendation. 'Do you see that man getting in – with a small dark beard – light overcoat? Follow him, see what he does and where he goes.'

'Is that all?' asked Mr Rowland. 'What do I——'

She interrupted him.

'Further instructions will be sent to you. Watch him – and guard this.' She thrust a small sealed packet into his hand. 'Guard it with your life. It's the key to everything.'

The train went on. Mr Rowland remained staring out of

the window, watching Elizabeth's tall, graceful figure threading its way down the platform. In his hand he clutched the small sealed packet.

The rest of his journey was both monotonous and uneventful. The train was a slow one. It stopped everywhere. At every station, George's head shot out of the window, in case his quarry should alight. Occasionally he strolled up and down the platform when the wait promised to be a long one, and reassured himself that the man was still there.

The eventual destination of the train was Portsmouth, and it was there that the black-bearded traveller alighted. He made his way to a small second-class hotel where he booked a room. Mr Rowland also booked a room.

The rooms were in the same corridor, two doors from each other. The arrangement seemed satisfactory to George. He was a complete novice in the art of shadowing, but was anxious to acquit himself well, and justify Elizabeth's trust in him.

At dinner George was given a table not far from that of his quarry. The room was not full, and the majority of the diners George put down as commercial travellers, quiet respectable men who ate their food with appetite. Only one man attracted his special notice, a small man with ginger hair and moustache and a suggestion of horsiness in his apparel. He seemed to be interested in George also, and suggested a drink and a game of billiards when the meal had come to a close. But George had just espied the black-bearded man putting on his hat and overcoat, and declined politely. In another minute he was out in the street, gaining fresh insight into the difficult art of shadowing. The chase was a long and a weary one – and in the end it seemed to lead nowhere. After twisting and turning through the streets of Portsmouth for about four miles, the man returned to the hotel, George hard upon his heels. A faint doubt assailed the latter. Was it possible that the man was aware of his presence? As he debated this point, standing in the hall, the outer door was pushed open, and the little ginger man entered. Evidently he, too, had been out for a stroll.

George was suddenly aware that the beauteous damsel in the office was addressing him.

'Mr Rowland, isn't it? Two gentlemen have called to see you. Two foreign gentlemen. They are in the little room at the end of the passage.'

Somewhat astonished, George sought the room in question. Two men were sitting there, rose to their feet and bowed punctiliously.

'Mr Rowland? I have no doubt, sir, that you can guess our identity.'

George gazed from one to the other of them. The spokesman was the elder of the two, a grey-haired, pompous gentleman who spoke excellent English. The other was a tall, somewhat pimply young man, with a blonde Teutonic cast of countenance which was not rendered more attractive by the fierce scowl which he wore at the present moment.

Somewhat relieved to find that neither of his visitors was the old gentleman he had encountered at Waterloo, George assumed his most debonair manner.

'Pray sit down, gentlemen. I'm delighted to make your acquaintance. How about a drink?'

The elder man held up a protesting hand.

'Thank you, Lord Rowland – not for us. We have but a few brief moments – just time for you to answer one question.'

'It's very kind of you to elect me to the peerage,' said George. 'I'm sorry you won't have a drink. And what is this momentous question?'

'Lord Rowland, you left London in company with a certain lady. You arrived here alone. Where is the lady?'

George rose to his feet.

'I fail to understand the question,' he said coldly, speaking as much like the hero of a novel as he could. 'I have the honour to wish you good evening, gentlemen.'

'But you do understand it. You understand it perfectly,'

cried the younger man, breaking out suddenly. 'What have you done with Alexa?'

'Be calm, sir,' murmured the other. 'I beg of you to be calm.'

'I can assure you,' said George, 'that I know no lady of that name. There is some mistake.'

The older man was eyeing him keenly.

'That can hardly be,' he said dryly. 'I took the liberty of examining the hotel register. You entered yourself as Mr G. Rowland of Rowland's Castle.'

George was forced to blush.

'A – a little joke of mine,' he explained feebly.

'A somewhat poor subterfuge. Come, let us not beat about the bush. Where is her Highness?'

'If you mean Elizabeth——'

With a howl of rage the young man flung himself forward again.

'Insolent pig-dog! To speak of her thus.'

'I am referring,' said the other slowly, 'as you very well know, to the Grand Duchess Anastasia Sophia Alexandra Marie Helena Olga Elizabeth of Catonia.'

'Oh!' said Mr Rowland helplessly.

He tried to recall all that he had ever known of Catonia. It was, as far as he remembered, a small Balkan kingdom, and he seemed to remember something about a revolution having occurred there. He rallied himself with an effort.

'Evidently we mean the same person,' he said cheerfully, 'only *I* call her Elizabeth.'

'You will give me satisfaction for that,' snarled the younger man. 'We will fight.'

'Fight?'

'A duel.'

'I never fight duels,' said Mr Rowland firmly.

'Why not?' demanded the other unpleasantly.

'I'm too afraid of getting hurt.'

'Aha! is that so? Then I will at least pull your nose for you.'

The young man advanced fiercely. Exactly what happened was difficult to see, but he described a sudden semicircle in the air and fell to the ground with a heavy thud. He picked himself up in a dazed manner. Mr Rowland was smiling pleasantly.

'As I was saying,' he remarked. 'I'm always afraid of getting hurt. That's why I thought it well to learn ju-jitsu.'

There was a pause. The two foreigners looked doubtfully at this amiable looking young man, as though they suddenly realized that some dangerous quality lurked behind the pleasant nonchalance of his manner. The young Teuton was white with passion.

'You will repent this,' he hissed.

The older man retained his dignity.

'That is your last word, Lord Rowland? You refuse to tell us Her Highness's whereabouts?'

'I'm unaware of them myself.'

'You can hardly expect me to believe that.'

'I am afraid you are of an unbelieving nature, sir.'

The other merely shook his head, and murmuring: 'This is not the end. You will hear from us again,' the two men took their leave.

George passed his hand over his brow. Events were proceeding at a bewildering rate. He was evidently mixed up in a first-class European scandal.

'It might even mean another war,' said George hopefully, as he hunted round to see what had become of the man with the black beard.

To his great relief, he discovered him sitting in a corner of the commercial-room. George sat down in another corner. In about three minutes the black-bearded man got up and went up to bed. George followed and saw him go into his room and close the door. George heaved a sigh of relief.

'I need a night's rest,' he murmured. 'Need it badly.'

Then a dire thought struck him. Supposing the black-bearded man had realized that George was on his trail?

Supposing that he should slip away during the night whilst George himself was sleeping the sleep of the just? A few minutes reflection suggested to Mr Rowland a way of dealing with this difficulty. He unravelled one of his socks till he got a good length of neutral-coloured wool, then creeping quietly out of his room, he pasted one end of the wool to the farther side of the stranger's door with stamp paper, carrying the wool across it and along to his own room. There he hung the end with a small silver bell – a relic of last night's entertainment. He surveyed these arrangements with a good deal of satisfaction. Should the black-bearded man attempt to leave his room George would be instantly warned by the ringing of the bell.

This matter disposed of. George lost no time in seeking his couch. The small packet he placed carefully under his pillow. As he did so, he fell into a momentary brown study. His thoughts could have been translated thus:

'Anastasia Sophia Marie Alexandra Olga Elizabeth. Hang it all, I've missed out one. I wonder now——'

He was unable to go to sleep immediately, being tantalized with his failure to grasp the situation. What was it all about? What was the connection between the escaping Grand Duchess, the sealed packet and the black-bearded man? What was the Grand Duchess escaping from? Were the two foreigners aware that the sealed packet was in his possession? What was it likely to contain?

Pondering these matters, with an irritated sense that he was no nearer their solution, Mr Rowland fell asleep.

He was awakened by the faint jangle of a bell. Not one of those men who awake to instant action, it took him just a minute and a half to realize the situation. Then he jumped up, thrust on some slippers, and, opening the door with the utmost caution, slipped out into the corridor. A faint moving patch of shadow at the far end of the passage showed him the direction taken by his quarry. Moving as noiselessly as possible, Mr Rowland followed the trail. He was just in time to see the black-bearded man disappear into a bathroom. That was puzzling, particularly so as there was a bathroom just opposite his own room. Moving up close to the door, which was ajar, George peered through the crack. The man was on his knees by the side of the bath, doing something to the skirting board immediately behind it. He remained there for about five minutes, then he rose to his feet, and George beat a prudent retreat. Safe in the shadow of his own door, he watched the other pass and regain his own room.

'Good,' said George to himself. 'The mystery of the bathroom will be investigated tomorrow morning.'

He got into bed and slipped his hand under the pillow to assure himself that the precious packet was still there. In another minute, he was scattering the bedclothes in a panic. The packet was gone!

It was a sadly chastened George who sat consuming eggs and bacon the following morning. He had failed Elizabeth. He had allowed the precious packet she had entrusted to his charge to be taken from him, and the 'Mystery of the Bathroom' was miserably inadequate. Yes, undoubtedly George had made a mutt of himself.

After breakfast he strolled upstairs again. A chambermaid was standing in the passage looking perplexed.

'Anything wrong, my dear?' said George kindly.

'It's the gentleman here, sir. He asked to be called at half-past eight, and I can't get any answer and the door's locked.'

'You don't say so,' said George.

An uneasy feeling arose in his own breast. He hurried into his room. Whatever plans he was forming were instantly brushed aside by a most unexpected sight. There on the dressing-table was the little package which had been stolen from him the night before!

George picked it up and examined it. Yes, it was undoubtedly the same. But the seals had been broken. After a minute's hesitation, he unwrapped it. If other people had seen its contents there was no reason why he should not see them also. Besides, it was possible that the contents had been abstracted. The unwound paper revealed a small cardboard box, such as jewellers use. George opened it. Inside nestling on a bed of cotton wool, was a plain gold wedding ring.

He picked it up and examined it. There was no inscription inside – nothing whatever to mark it out from any other wedding ring. George dropped his head into his hands with a groan.

'Lunacy,' he murmured. 'That's what it is. Stark, staring lunacy. There's no sense anywhere.'

Suddenly he remembered the chambermaid's statement, and at the same time he observed that there was a broad parapet outside the window. It was not a feat he would ordinarily have attempted, but he was so aflame with curiosity and anger that he was in the mood to make light of difficulties. He sprang upon the window sill. A few seconds later he was peering in at the window of the room occupied by the black-bearded man. The window was open and the room was empty. A little farther along was a fire escape. It was clear how the quarry had taken his departure.

George jumped in through the window. The missing man's effects were still scattered about. There might be some clue amongst them to shed light on George's perplexities. He began to hunt about, starting with the contents of a battered kit-bag.

It was a sound that arrested his search – a very slight sound, but a sound indubitably in the room. George's glance leapt to the big wardrobe. He sprang up and wrenched open the door. As he did so, a man jumped out from it and went rolling over the floor locked in George's embrace. He was no mean antagonist. All George's special tricks availed very little. They fell apart at length in sheer exhaustion, and for the first time George saw who his adversary was. It was the little man with the ginger moustache!

'Who the devil are you?' demanded George.

For answer the other drew out a card and handed it to him. George read it aloud.

'Detective-Inspector Jarrold, Scotland Yard.'

'That's right, sir. And you'd do well to tell me all you know about this business.'

'I would, would I?' said George thoughtfully. 'Do you know, inspector, I believe you're right. Shall we adjourn to a more cheerful spot?'

In a quiet corner of the bar George unfolded his soul. Inspector Jarrold listened sympathetically.

'Very puzzling, as you say, sir,' he remarked when George had finished. 'There's a lot as I can't make head or tail of myself, but there's one or two points I can clear up for you. I was here after Mardenberg (your black-bearded friend) and your turning up and watching him the way you did made me suspicious. I couldn't place you. I slipped into your room last night when you were out of it, and it was I who sneaked the little packet from under your pillow. When I opened it and found it wasn't what I was after, I took the first opportunity of returning it to your room.'

'That makes things a little clearer certainly,' said George thoughtfully. 'I seem to have made rather an ass of myself all through.'

'I wouldn't say that, sir. You did uncommon well for a beginner. You say you visited the bathroom this morning and took away what was concealed behind the skirting board?'

'Yes. But it's only a rotten love letter,' said George gloomily. 'Dash it all, I didn't mean to go nosing out the poor fellow's private life.'

'Would you mind letting me see it, sir?'

George took a folded letter from his pocket and passed it to the inspector. The latter unfolded it.

'As you say, sir. But I rather fancy that if you drew lines from one dotted *i* to another, you'd get a different result.

Why, bless you, sir, this is a plan of the Portsmouth harbour defences.'

'What?'

'Yes. We've had our eye on the gentleman for some time. But he was too sharp for us. Got a woman to do most of the dirty work.'

'A woman?' said George, in a faint voice. 'What was her name?'

'She goes by a good many, sir. Most usually known as Betty Brighteyes. A remarkably good-looking young woman she is.'

'Betty – Brighteyes,' said George. 'Thank you, inspector.'

'Excuse me, sir, but you're not looking well?'

'I'm not well. I'm very ill. In fact, I think I'd better take the first train back to town.'

The inspector looked at his watch.

'That will be a slow train, I'm afraid, sir. Better wait for the express.'

'It doesn't matter,' said George gloomily. 'No train could be slower than the one I came down by yesterday.'

Seated once more in a first-class carriage, George leisurely perused the day's news. Suddenly he sat bolt upright and stared at the sheet in front of him.

'A romantic wedding took place yesterday in London when Lord Roland Gaigh, second son of the Marquis of Axminster, was married to the Grand Duchess Anastasia of Catonia. The ceremony was kept a profound secret. The Grand Duchess has been living in Paris with her uncle since the upheaval in Catonia. She met Lord Roland when he was secretary to the British Embassy in Catonia and their attachment dates from that time.'

'Well, I'm——'

Mr Rowland could not think of anything strong enough to express his feelings. He continued to stare into space. The train stopped at a small station and a lady got in. She sat down opposite him.

'Good morning, George,' she said sweetly.

'Good heavens!' cried George. 'Elizabeth!'

She smiled at him. She was, if possible, lovelier than ever.

'Look here,' cried George, clutching his head. 'For God's sake tell me. Are you the Grand Duchess Anastasia, or are you Betty Brighteyes?'

She stared at him.

'I'm not either. I'm Elizabeth Gaigh. I can tell you all about it now. And I've got to apologize too. You see, Roland (that's my brother) has always been in love with Alexa——'

'Meaning the Grand Duchess?'

'Yes, that's what the family call her. Well, as I say, Roland was always in love with her, and she with him. And then the revolution came, and Alexa was in Paris, and they were just going to fix it up when old Stürm, the chancellor, came along and insisted on carrying off Alexa and forcing her to marry Prince Karl, her cousin, a horrid pimply person——'

'I fancy I've met him,' said George.

'Whom she simply hates. And old Prince Osric, her uncle, forbade her to see Roland again. So she ran away to England, and I came up to town and met her, and we wired to Roland who was in Scotland. And just at the very last minute, when we were driving to the Registry Office in a taxi, whom should we meet in another taxi face to face, but old Prince Osric. Of course he followed us, and we were at our wits' end what to do because he'd have made the most fearful scene, and, anyway, he is her guardian. Then I had the brilliant idea of changing places. You can practically see nothing of a girl nowadays but the tip of her nose. I put on Alexa's red hat and brown wrap coat, and she put on my grey. Then we told the taxi to go to Waterloo, and I skipped out there and hurried into the station. Old Osric followed the red hat all right, without a thought for the other occupant of the taxi sitting huddled up inside, but of course it wouldn't do for him to see my face. So I just bolted into your carriage and threw myself on your mercy.'

'I've got that all right,' said George. 'It's the rest of it.'

'I know. That's what I've got to apologize about. I hope you won't be awfully cross. You see, you looked so keen on its being a real mystery – like in books, that I really couldn't resist the temptation. I picked out a rather sinister looking man on the platform and told you to follow him. And then I thrust the parcel on you.'

'Containing a wedding ring.'

'Yes. Alexa and I bought that, because Roland wasn't due to arrive from Scotland until just before the wedding. And of course I knew that by the time I got to London they wouldn't want it – they would have had to use a curtain ring or something.'

'I see,' said George. 'It's like all these things – so simple when you know! Allow me, Elizabeth.'

He stripped off her left glove, and uttered a sigh of relief at the sight of the bare third finger.

'That's all right,' he remarked. 'That ring won't be wasted after all.'

'Oh!' cried Elizabeth; 'but I don't know anything about you.'

'You know how nice I am,' said George. 'By the way, it has just occurred to me, you are the Lady Elizabeth Gaigh, of course.'

'Oh! George, are you a snob?'

'As a matter of fact, I am, rather. My best dream was one where King George borrowed half a crown from me to see him over the weekend. But I was thinking of my uncle – the one from whom I am estranged. He's a frightful snob. When he knows I'm going to marry you, and that we'll have a title in the family, he'll make me a partner at once!'

'Oh! George, is he very rich?'

'Elizabeth, are you mercenary?'

'Very. I adore spending money. But I was thinking of father. Five daughters, full of beauty and blue blood. He's just yearning for a rich son-in-law.'

'H'm,' said George. 'It will be one of those marriages made in Heaven and approved on earth. Shall we live at Rowland's Castle? They'd be sure to make me Lord Mayor with you for a wife. Oh! Elizabeth, darling, it's probably contravening the company's by-laws, but I simply must kiss you!'

Magnolia Blossom

Vincent Easton was waiting under the clock at Victoria Station. Now and then he glanced up at it uneasily. He thought to himself: 'How many other men have waited here for a woman who didn't come?'

A sharp pang shot through him. Supposing that Theo didn't come, that she had changed her mind? Women did that sort of thing. Was he sure of her – had he ever been sure of her? Did he really know anything at all about her? Hadn't she puzzled him from the first? There had seemed to be two women – the lovely, laughing creature who was Richard Darrell's wife, and the other – silent, mysterious, who had walked by his side in the garden of Haymer's Close. Like a magnolia flower – that was how he thought of her – perhaps because it was under the magnolia tree that they had tasted their first rapturous, incredulous kiss. The air had been sweet with the scent of magnolia bloom, and one or two petals, velvety-soft and fragrant, had floated down, resting on that upturned face that was as creamy and as soft and as silent as they. Magnolia blossom – exotic, fragrant, mysterious.

That had been a fortnight ago – the second day he had met her. And now he was waiting for her to come to him forever. Again incredulity shot through him. She wouldn't come. How could he ever have believed it? It would be giving up so much. The beautiful Mrs Darrell couldn't do this sort of thing quietly. It was bound to be a nine days' wonder, a far-reaching scandal that would never quite be forgotten. There were better, more expedient ways of doing these things – a discreet divorce, for instance.

But they had never thought of that for a moment – at least he had not. Had she, he wondered? He had never known anything of her thoughts. He had asked her to come away with him almost timorously – for after all, what was he? Nobody in particular – one of a thousand orange-growers in the Transvaal. What a life to take her to – after the brilliance of London! And yet, since he wanted her so desperately, he must needs ask.

She had consented very quietly, with no hesitations or protests, as though it were the simplest thing in the world that he was asking her.

'Tomorrow?' he had said, amazed, almost unbelieving.

And she had promised in that soft, broken voice that was so different from the laughing brilliance of her social manner. He had compared her to a diamond when he first saw her – a thing of flashing fire, reflecting light from a hundred facets. But at that first touch, that first kiss, she had changed miraculously to the clouded softness of a pearl – a pearl like a magnolia blossom, creamy-pink.

She had promised. And now he was waiting for her to fulfil that promise.

He looked again at the clock. If she did not come soon, they would miss the train.

Sharply a wave of reaction set in. She wouldn't come! Of course she wouldn't come. Fool that he had been ever to expect it! What were promises? He would find a letter when he got back to his rooms – explaining, protesting, saying all the things that women do when they are excusing themselves for lack of courage.

He felt anger – anger and the bitterness of frustration.

Then he saw her coming towards him down the platform,

a faint smile on her face. She walked slowly, without haste or fluster, as one who had all eternity before her. She was in black – soft black that clung, with a little black hat that framed the wonderful creamy pallor of her face.

He found himself grasping her hand, muttering stupidly:

'So you've come – you have come. After all!'

'Of course.'

How calm her voice sounded! How calm!

'I thought you wouldn't,' he said, releasing her hand and breathing hard.

Her eyes opened – wide, beautiful eyes. There was wonder in them, the simple wonder of a child.

'Why?'

He didn't answer. Instead he turned aside and requisitioned a passing porter. They had not much time. The next few minutes were all bustle and confusion. Then they were sitting in their reserved compartment and the drab houses of southern London were drifting by them.

Theodora Darrell was sitting opposite him. At last she was his. And he knew now how incredulous, up to the very last minute, he had been. He had not dared to let himself believe. That magical, elusive quality about her had frightened him. It had seemed impossible that she should ever belong to him.

Now the suspense was over. The irrevocable step was taken. He looked across at her. She lay back in the corner, quite still. The faint smile lingered on her lips, her eyes were cast down, the long, black lashes swept the creamy curve of her cheek.

He thought: 'What's in her mind now? What is she thinking of? Me? Her husband? What does she think about him anyway? Did she care for him once? Or did she never care? Does she hate him, or is she indifferent to him?' And with a pang the thought swept through him: 'I don't know. I never shall know. I love her, and I don't know anything about her – what she thinks or what she feels.'

His mind circled round the thought of Theodora Darrell's husband. He had known plenty of married women who were only too ready to talk about their husbands – of how they were misunderstood by them, of how their finer feelings were ignored. Vincent Easton reflected cynically that it was one of the best-known opening gambits.

But except casually, Theo had never spoken of Richard Darrell. Easton knew of him what everybody knew. He was a popular man, handsome, with an engaging, carefree manner. Everybody liked Darrell. His wife always seemed on excellent terms with him. But that proved nothing, Vincent reflected. Theo was well-bred – she would not air her grievances in public.

And between them, no word had passed. From that second evening of their meeting, when they had walked together in the garden, silent, their shoulders touching, and he had felt the faint tremor that shook her at his touch, there had been no explainings, a dumb, trembling creature, shorn of all that hard brilliance which, together with her cream-and-rose beauty, had made her famous. Never once had she spoken of her husband. Vincent had been thankful for that at the time. He had been glad to be spared the arguments of a woman who wished to assure herself and her lover that they were justified in yielding to their love.

Yet now the tacit conspiracy of silence worried him. He had again that panic-stricken sense of knowing nothing about this strange creature who was willingly linking her life to his. He was afraid.

In the impulse to reassure himself, he bent forward and laid a hand on the black-clad knee opposite him. He felt once again the faint tremor that shook her, and he reached up for her hand. Bending forward, he kissed the palm, a long, lingering kiss. He felt the response of her fingers on his and, looking up, met her eyes, and was content.

He leaned back in his seat. For the moment, he wanted no

more. They were together. She was his. And presently he said in a light, almost bantering tone:

'You're very silent?'

'Am I?'

'Yes.' He waited a minute, then said in a graver tone: 'You're sure you don't – regret?'

Her eyes opened wide at that. 'Oh, no!'

He did not doubt the reply. There was an assurance of sincerity behind it.

'What are you thinking about? I want to know.'

In a low voice she answered: 'I think I'm afraid.'

'Afraid?'

'Of happiness.'

He moved over beside her then, held her to him and kissed the softness of her face and neck.

'I love you,' he said. 'I love you – love you.'

Her answer was in the clinging of her body, the abandon of her lips.

Then he moved back to his own corner. He picked up a magazine and so did she. Every now and then, over the top of the magazines, their eyes met. Then they smiled.

II

He felt anger – anger and the bitterness of frustration.

They arrived at Dover just after five. They were to spend the night there, and cross to the Continent on the following day. Theo entered their sitting room in the hotel with Vincent close behind her. He had a couple of evening papers in his hand which he threw down on the table. Two of the hotel servants brought in the luggage and withdrew.

Theo turned from the window where she had been standing looking out. In another minute they were in each other's arms.

There was a discreet tap on the door and they drew apart again.

'Damn it all,' said Vincent, 'it doesn't seem as though we are ever going to be alone.'

Theo smiled. 'It doesn't look like it,' she said softly. Sitting down on the sofa, she picked up one of the papers.

The knock proved to be a waiter bearing tea. He laid it on the table, drawing the latter up to the sofa on which Theo was sitting, cast a deft glance round, inquired if there were anything further, and withdrew.

Vincent, who had gone into the adjoining room, came back into the sitting room.

'Now for tea,' he said cheerily, but stopped suddenly in the middle of the room. 'Anything wrong?' he asked.

Theo was sitting bolt upright on the sofa. She was staring in front of her with dazed eyes, and her face had gone deathly white.

Vincent took a quick step towards her.

'What is it, sweetheart?'

For answer she held out the paper to him, her finger pointing to the headline.

Vincent took the paper from her. 'FAILURE OF HOBSON, JEKYLL AND LUCAS,' he read. The name of the big city firm conveyed nothing to him at the moment, though he had an irritating conviction in the back of his mind that it ought to do so. He looked inquiringly at Theo.

'Richard is Hobson, Jekyll and Lucas,' she explained.

'Your husband?'

'Yes.'

Vincent returned to the paper and read the bald information it conveyed carefully. Phrases such as 'sudden crash,' 'serious revelations to follow,' 'other houses affected' struck him disgreeably.

Roused by a movement, he looked up. Theo was adjusting her little black hat in front of the mirror. She turned at the movement he made. Her eyes looked steadily into his.

'Vincent – I must go to Richard.'

He sprang up.

'Theo – don't be absurd.'

She repeated mechanically:

'I must go to Richard.'

'But, my dear –'

She made a gesture towards the paper on the floor.

'That means ruin – bankruptcy. I can't choose this day of all others to leave him.'

'You had left him before you heard of this. Be reasonable!'

She shook her head mournfully.

'You don't understand. I must go to Richard.'

And from that he could not move her. Strange that a creature so soft, so pliant, could be so unyielding. After the first, she did not argue. She let him say what he had to say unhindered. He held her in his arms, seeking to break her will by enslaving her senses, but though her soft mouth returned his kisses, he felt in her something aloof and invincible that withstood all his pleadings.

He let her go at last, sick and weary of the vain endeavour. From pleading he had turned to bitterness, reproaching her with never having loved him. That, too, she took in silence, without protest, her face, dumb and pitiful, giving the lie to his words. Rage mastered him in the end; he hurled at her every cruel word he could think of, seeking only to bruise and batter her to her knees.

At last the words gave out; there was nothing more to say. He sat, his head in his hands, staring down at the red pile carpet. By the door, Theodora stood, a black shadow with a white face.

It was all over.

She said quietly: 'Goodbye, Vincent.'

He did not answer.

The door opened – and shut again.

*

III

The Darrells lived in a house in Chelsea – an intriguing, old-world house, standing in a little garden of its own. Up the front of the house grew a magnolia tree, smutty, dirty, begrimed, but still a magnolia.

Theo looked up at it, as she stood on the doorstep some three hours later. A sudden smile twisted her mouth in pain.

She went straight to the study at the back of the house. A man was pacing up and down in the room – a young man, with a handsome face and a haggard expression.

He gave an ejaculation of relief as she came in.

'Thank God you've turned up, Theo. They said you'd taken your luggage with you and gone off out of town somewhere.'

'I heard the news and came back.'

Richard Darrell put an arm about her and drew her to the couch. They sat down upon it side by side. Theo drew herself free of the encircling arm in what seemed a perfectly natural manner.

'How bad is it, Richard?' she asked quietly.

'Just as bad as it can be – and that's saying a lot.'

'Tell me!'

He began to walk up and down again as he talked. Theo sat and watched him. He was not to know that every now and then the room went dim, and his voice faded from her hearing, while another room in a hotel at Dover came clearly before her eyes.

Nevertheless she managed to listen intelligently enough. He came back and sat down on the couch by her.

'Fortunately,' he ended, 'they can't touch your marriage settlement. The house is yours also.'

Theo nodded thoughtfully.

'We shall have that at any rate,' she said. 'Then things will not be too bad? It means a fresh start, that is all.'

'Oh! Quite so. Yes.'

But his voice did not ring true, and Theo thought suddenly: 'There's something else. He hasn't told me everything.'

'There's nothing more, Richard?' she said gently. 'Nothing worse?'

He hesitated for just half a second, then: 'Worse? What should there be?'

'I don't know,' said Theo.

'It'll be all right,' said Richard, speaking more as though to reassure himself than Theo. 'Of course, it'll be all right.'

He flung an arm about her suddenly.

'I'm glad you're here,' he said. 'It'll be all right now that you're here. Whatever else happens. I've got you, haven't I?'

She said gently: 'Yes, you've got me.' And this time she left his arm round her.

He kissed her and held her close to him, as though in some strange way he derived comfort from her nearness.

'I've got you, Theo,' he said again presently, and she answered as before: 'Yes, Richard.'

He slipped from the couch to the floor at her feet.

'I'm tired out,' he said fretfully. 'My God, it's been a day. Awful! I don't know what I should do if you weren't here. After all, one's wife is one's wife, isn't she?'

She did not speak, only bowed her head in assent.

He laid his head on her lap. The sigh he gave was like that of a tired child.

Theo thought again: 'There's something he hasn't told me. What is it?'

Mechanically her hand dropped to his smooth, dark head, and she stroked it gently, as a mother might comfort a child.

Richard murmured vaguely:

'It'll be all right now you're here. You won't let me down.'

His breathing grew slow and even. He slept. Her hand still smoothed his head.

But her eyes looked steadily into the darkness in front of her, seeing nothing.

*

'Don't you think, Richard,' said Theodora, 'that you'd better tell me everything?'

It was three days later. They were in the drawing room before dinner.

Richard started, and flushed.

'I don't know what you mean,' he parried.

'Don't you?'

He shot a quick glance at her.

'Of course there are – well – details.'

'I ought to know everything, don't you think, if I am to help?'

He looked at her strangely.

'What makes you think I want you to help?'

She was a little astonished.

'My dear Richard, I'm your wife.'

He smiled suddenly, the old, attractive, carefree smile.

'So you are, Theo. And a very good-looking wife, too. I never could stand ugly women.'

He began walking up and down the room, as was his custom when something was worrying him.

'I won't deny you're right in a way,' he said presently. 'There is something.'

He broke off.

'Yes?'

'It's so damned hard to explain things of this kind to women. They get hold of the wrong end of the stick – fancy a thing is – well, what it isn't.'

Theo said nothing.

'You see,' went on Richard, 'the law's one thing and right and wrong are quite another. I may do a thing that's perfectly right and honest, but the law wouldn't take the same view of it. Nine times out of ten, everything pans out all right, and the tenth time you – well, hit a snag.'

Theo began to understand. She thought to herself: 'Why am I not surprised? Did I always know, deep down, that he wasn't straight?'

Richard went on talking. He explained himself at unnecessary lengths. Theo was content for him to cloak the actual details of the affair in this mantle of verbosity. The matter concerned a large tract of South African property. Exactly what Richard had done, she was not concerned to know. Morally, he assured her, everything was fair and above board; legally – well, there was; no getting away from the fact, he had rendered himself liable to criminal prosecution.

He kept shooting quick glances at his wife as he talked. He was nervous and uncomfortable. And still he excused himself and tried to explain away that which a child might have seen in its naked truth. Then finally in a burst of justification, he broke down. Perhaps Theo's eyes, momentarily scornful, had something to do with it. He sank down in a chair by the fireplace, his head in his hands.

'There it is, Theo,' he said brokenly. 'What are you going to do about it?'

She came over to him with scarcely a moment's pause and, kneeling down by the chair, put her face against his.

'What can be done, Richard? What can we do?'

He caught her to him.

'You mean it? You'll stick to me?'

'Of course. My dear, of course.'

He said, moved to sincerity in spite of himself: 'I'm a thief, Theo. That's what it means, shorn of fine language – just a thief.'

'Then I'm a thief's wife, Richard. We'll sink or swim together.'

They were silent for a little while. Presently Richard recovered something of his jaunty manner.

'You know, Theo, I've got a plan, but we'll talk of that later. It's just on dinnertime. We must go and change. Put on that creamy thingummybob of yours, you know – the Caillot model.'

Theo raised her eyebrows quizzically.

'For an evening at home?'

'Yes, yes, I know. But I like it. Put it on, there's a good girl. It cheers me up to see you looking your best.'

Theo came down to dinner in the Caillot. It was a creation in creamy brocade, with a faint pattern of gold running through it and an undernote of pale pink to give warmth to the cream. It was cut daringly low in the back, and nothing could have been better-designed to show off the dazzling whiteness of Theo's neck and shoulders. She was truly now a magnolia flower.

Richard's eye rested upon her in warm approval. 'Good girl. You know, you look simply stunning in that dress.'

They went in to dinner. Throughout the evening Richard was nervous and unlike himself, joking and laughing about nothing at all, as if in a vain attempt to shake off his cares. Several times Theo tried to lead him back to the subject they had been discussing before, but he edged away from it.

Then suddenly, as she rose to go to bed, he came to the point.

'No, don't go yet. I've something to say. You know, about this miserable business.'

She sat down again.

He began talking rapidly. With a bit of luck, the whole thing could be hushed up. He had covered his tracks fairly well. So long as certain papers didn't get into the receiver's hands –

He stopped significantly.

'Papers?' asked Theo perplexedly. 'You mean you will destroy them?'

Richard made a grimace.

'I'd destroy them fast enough if I could get hold of them. That's the devil of it all!'

'Who has them, then?'

'A man we both know – Vincent Easton.'

A very faint exclamation escaped Theo. She forced it back, but Richard had noticed it.

'I've suspected he knew something of the business all along. That's why I've asked him here a good bit. You may remember that I asked you to be nice to him?'

'I remember,' said Theo.

'Somehow I never seem to have got on really friendly terms with him. Don't know why. But he likes you. I should say he likes you a good deal.'

Theo said in a very clear voice: 'He does.'

'Ah!' said Richard appreciatively. 'That's good. Now you see what I'm driving at. I'm convinced that if you went to Vincent Easton and asked him to give you those papers, he wouldn't refuse. Pretty woman, you know – all that sort of thing.'

'I can't do that,' said Theo quickly.

'Nonsense.'

'It's out of the question.'

The red came slowly out in blotches on Richard's face. She saw that he was angry.

'My dear girl, I don't think you quite realize the position. If this comes out, I'm liable to go to prison. It's ruin – disgrace.'

'Vincent Easton will not use those papers against you. I am sure of that.'

'That's not quite the point. He mayn't realize that they incriminate me. It's only taken in conjunction with – with my affairs – with the figures they're bound to find. Oh! I can't go into details. He'll ruin me without knowing what he's doing unless somebody puts the position before him.'

'You can do that yourself, surely. Write to him.'

'A fat lot of good that would be! No, Theo, we've only got one hope. You're the trump card. You're my wife. You must help me. Go to Easton tonight –'

A cry broke from Theo.

'Not tonight. Tomorrow perhaps.'

'My God, Theo, can't you realize things? Tomorrow may be too late. If you could go now – at once – to Easton's rooms.' He saw her flinch, and tried to reassure her. 'I know, my dear girl, I know. It's a beastly thing to do. But it's life or death. Theo, you won't fail me? You said you'd do anything to help me –'

Theo heard herself speaking in a hard, dry voice. 'Not this thing. There are reasons.'

'It's life or death, Theo. I mean it. See here.'

He snapped open a drawer of the desk and took out a revolver. If there was something theatrical about that action, it escaped her notice.

'It's that or shooting myself. I can't face the racket. If you won't do as I ask you, I'll be a dead man before morning. I swear to you solemnly that that's the truth.'

Theo gave a low cry. 'No, Richard, not that!'

'Then help me.'

He flung the revolver down on the table and knelt by her side. 'Theo, my darling – if you love me – if you've ever loved me – do this for me. You're my wife, Theo. I've no one else to turn to.'

On and on his voice went, murmuring, pleading. And at last Theo heard her own voice saying: 'Very well – yes.'

Richard took her to the door and put her into a taxi.

IV

'Theo!'

Vincent Easton sprang up in incredulous delight. She stood in the doorway. Her wrap of white ermine was hanging from her shoulders. Never, Easton thought, had she looked so beautiful.

'You've come after all.'

She put out a hand to stop him as he came towards her.

'No, Vincent, this isn't what you think.'

She spoke in a low, hurried voice.

'I'm here from my husband. He thinks there are some papers which may – do him harm. I have come to ask you to give them to me.'

Vincent stood very still, looking at her. Then he gave a short laugh.

'So that's it, is it? I thought Hobson, Jekyll and Lucas sounded familiar the other day, but I couldn't place them at the minute. Didn't know your husband was connected with the firm. Things have been going wrong there for some time. I was commissioned to look into the matter. I suspected some underling. Never thought of the man at the top.'

Theo said nothing. Vincent looked at her curiously.

'It makes no difference to you, this?' he asked. 'That – well, to put it plainly, that your husband's a swindler?'

She shook her head.

'It beats me,' said Vincent. Then he added quietly: 'Will you wait a minute or two? I will get the papers.'

Theo sat down in a chair. He went into the other room. Presently he returned and delivered a small package into her hand.

'Thank you,' said Theo. 'Have you a match?'

Taking the matchbox her proffered, she knelt down by the fireplace. When the papers were reduced to a pile of ashes, she stood up.

'Thank you,' she said again.

'Not at all,' he answered formally. 'Let me get you a taxi.'

He put her into it, saw her drive away. A strange, formal little interview. After the first, they had not even dared look at each other. Well, that was that, the end. He would go away, abroad, try and forget.

Theo leaned her head out of the window and spoke to the taxi driver. She could not go back at once to the house in Chelsea. She must have a breathing space. Seeing Vincent again had shaken her horribly. If only – if only. But she pulled herself up. Love for her husband she had none – but she owed him loyalty. He was down, she must stick by him. Whatever else he might have done, he loved her; his offence had been committed against society, not against her.

The taxi meandered on through the wide streets of Hampstead. They came out on the heath, and a breath of cool, invigorating air fanned Theo's cheeks. She had herself in hand again now. The taxi sped back towards Chelsea.

Richard came out to meet her in the hall.

'Well,' he demanded, 'you've been a long time.'

'Have I?'

'Yes – a very long time. Is it – all right?'

He followed her, a cunning look in his eyes. His hands were shaking.

'It's – it's all right, eh?' he said again.

'I burnt them myself.'

'Oh!'

She went on into the study, sinking into a big armchair. Her face was dead white and her whole body drooped with fatigue. She thought to herself: 'If only I could go to sleep now and never, never wake up again!'

Richard was watching her. His glance, shy, furtive, kept coming and going. She noticed nothing. She was beyond noticing.

'It went off quite all right, eh?'

'I've told you so.'

'You're sure they were the right papers? Did you look?'

'No.'

'But then –'

'I'm sure, I tell you. Don't bother me, Richard. I can't bear any more tonight.'

Richard shifted nervously.

'No, no. I see.'

He fidgeted about the room. Presently he came over to her, laid a hand on her shoulder. She shook it off.

'Don't touch me.' She tried to laugh. 'I'm sorry, Richard. My nerves are on edge. I feel I can't bear to be touched.'

'I know. I understand.'

Again he wandered up and down.

'Theo,' he burst out suddenly. 'I'm damned sorry.'

'What?' She looked up, vaguely startled.

'I oughtn't to have let you go there at this time of night. I never dreamed that you'd be subjected to any – unpleasantness.'

'Unpleasantness?' She laughed. The word seemed to amuse her. 'You don't know! Oh, Richard, you don't know!'

'I don't know what?'

She said very gravely, looking straight in front of her: 'What this night has cost me.'

'My God! Theo! I never meant – You – you did that, for me? The swine! Theo – Theo – I couldn't have known. I couldn't have guessed. My God!'

He was kneeling by her now stammering, his arms round her, and she turned and looked at him with faint surprise, as though his words had at last really penetrated to her attention.

'I – I never meant –'

'You never meant what, Richard?'

Her voice startled him.

'Tell me. What was it that you never meant?'

'Theo, don't let us speak of it. I don't want to know. I never want to think of it.'

She was staring at him, wide awake now, with every faculty alert. Her words came clear and distinct:

'You never meant – What do you think happened?'

'It didn't happen, Theo. Let's say it didn't happen.'

And still she stared, till the truth began to come to her.

'You think that –'

'I don't want –'

She interrupted him: 'You think that Vincent Easton asked a price for those letters? You think that I – paid him?'

Richard said weakly and unconvincingly: 'I – I never dreamed he was that kind of man.'

*

V

'Didn't you?' She looked at him searchingly. His eyes fell before hers. 'Why did you ask me to put on this dress this evening? Why did you send me there alone at this time of night? You guessed he – cared for me. You wanted to save your skin – save it at any cost – even at the cost of my honour.' She got up.

'I see now. You meant that from the beginning – or at least you saw it as a possibility, and it didn't deter you.'

'Theo –'

'You can't deny it. Richard, I thought I knew all there was to know about you years ago. I've known almost from the first that you weren't straight as regards the world. But I thought you were straight with me.'

'Theo –'

'Can you deny what I've just been saying?'

He was silent in spite of himself.

'Listen, Richard. There is something I must tell you. Three days ago when this blow fell on you, the servants told you I was away – gone to the country. That was only partly true. I had gone away with Vincent Easton –'

Richard made an inarticulate sound. She held out a hand to stop him.

'Wait. We were at Dover. I saw a paper – I realized what had happened. Then, as you know, I came back.'

She paused.

Richard caught her by the wrist. His eyes burnt into hers.

'You came back – in time?'

Theo gave a short, bitter laugh.

'Yes, I came back, as you say, "in time", Richard.'

Her husband relinquished his hold on her arm. He stood by the mantelpiece, his head thrown back. He looked handsome and rather noble.

'In that case,' he said, 'I can forgive.'

'I cannot.'

The two words came crisply. They had the semblance and the effect of a bomb in the quiet room. Richard started forward, staring, his jaw dropped with an almost ludicrous effect.

'You – er – what did you say, Theo?'

'I said I cannot forgive! In leaving you for another man, I sinned – not technically, perhaps, but in intention, which is the same thing. But if I sinned, I sinned through love. You, too, have not been faithful to me since our marriage. Oh, yes, I know. That I forgave you, because I really believed in your love for me. But the thing you have done tonight is different. It is an ugly thing, Richard – a thing no woman should forgive. You sold me, your own wife, to purchase safety!'

She picked up her wrap and turned towards the door.

'Theo,' he stammered out, 'where are you going?'

She looked back over her shoulder at him.

'We all have to pay in this life, Richard. For my sin I must pay in loneliness. For yours – well, you gambled with the thing you love, and you have lost it!'

'You are going?'

She drew a long breath.

'To freedom. There is nothing to bind me here.'

He heard the door shut. Ages passed, or was it a few minutes? Something fluttered down outside the window – the last of the magnolia petals, soft, fragrant.

Jane in Search of a Job

Jane Cleveland rustled the pages of the *Daily Leader* and sighed. A deep sigh that came from the innermost recesses of her being. She looked with distaste at the marble-topped table, the poached egg on toast which reposed on it, and the small pot of tea. Not because she was not hungry. That was far from being the case. Jane was extremely hungry. At that moment she felt like consuming a pound and a half of well-cooked beefsteak, with chip potatoes, and possibly French beans. The whole washed down with some more exciting vintage than tea.

But young women whose exchequers are in a parlous condition cannot be choosers. Jane was lucky to be able to order a poached egg and a pot of tea. It seemed unlikely that she would be able to do so tomorrow. That is unless——

She turned once more to the advertisement columns of the *Daily Leader*. To put it plainly, Jane was out of a job, and the position was becoming acute. Already the genteel lady who presided over the shabby boarding-house was looking askance at this particular young woman.

'And yet,' said Jane to herself, throwing up her chin indignantly, which was a habit of hers. 'And yet I'm intelligent and good-looking and well educated. What more does any one want?'

According to the *Daily Leader*, they seemed to want shorthand typists of vast experience, managers for business houses with a little capital to invest, ladies to share in the profits of poultry farming (here again a little capital was required), and innumerable cooks, housemaids and parlourmaids – particularly parlourmaids.

'I wouldn't mind being a parlourmaid,' said Jane to herself. 'But there again, no one would take me without experience. I could go somewhere, I dare say, as a Willing Young Girl – but they don't pay willing young girls anything to speak of.'

She sighed again, propped the paper up in front of her, and attacked the poached egg with all the vigour of healthy youth.

When the last mouthful had been despatched, she turned the paper, and studied the Agony and Personal column whilst she drank her tea. The Agony column was always the last hope.

Had she but possessed a couple of thousand pounds, the thing would have been easy enough. There were at least seven unique opportunities – all yielding not less than three thousand a year. Jane's lip curled a little.

'If I had two thousand pounds,' she murmured, 'it wouldn't be easy to separate from it.'

She cast her eyes rapidly down to the bottom of the column and ascended with the ease born of long practice.

There was the lady who gave such wonderful prices for cast-off clothing. 'Ladies' wardrobes inspected at their own dwellings.' There were the gentlemen who bought ANYTHING – but principally TEETH. There were ladies of title going abroad who would dispose of their furs at a ridiculous figure. There was the distressed clergyman and the hard-working widow, and the disabled officer, all needing sums varying from fifty pounds to two thousand. And then suddenly Jane came to an abrupt halt. She put down her teacup and read the advertisement through again.

'There's a catch in it, of course,' she murmured. 'There

always is a catch in these sort of things. I shall have to be careful. But still——'

The advertisement which so intrigued Jane Cleveland ran as follows:

> If a young lady of twenty-five to thirty years of age, eyes dark blue, very fair hair, black lashes and brows, straight nose, slim figure, height five feet seven inches, good mimic and able to speak French, will call at 7 Endersleigh Street, between 5 and 6 p.m., she will hear of something to her advantage.

'Guileless Gwendolen, or why girls go wrong,' murmured Jane. 'I shall certainly have to be careful. But there are too many specifications, really, for that sort of thing. I wonder now. . . . Let us overhaul the catalogue.'

She proceeded to do so.

'Twenty-five to thirty – I'm twenty-six. Eyes dark blue, that's right. Hair very fair – black lashes and brows – all O.K. Straight nose? Ye-es – straight enough, anyway. It doesn't hook or turn up. And I've got a slim figure – slim even for nowadays. I'm only five feet six inches – but I could wear high heels. I *am* a good mimic – nothing wonderful, but I can copy people's voices, and I speak French like an angel or a Frenchwoman. In fact, I'm absolutely the goods. They ought to tumble over themselves with delight when I turn up. Jane Cleveland, go in and win.'

Resolutely Jane tore out the advertisement and placed it in her handbag. Then she demanded her bill, with a new briskness in her voice.

At ten minutes to five Jane was reconnoitring in the neighbourhood of Endersleigh Street. Endersleigh Street itself is a small street sandwiched between two larger streets in the neighbourhood of Oxford Circus. It is drab, but respectable.

No. 7 seemed in no way different from the neighbouring

houses. It was composed like they were of offices. But looking up at it, it dawned upon Jane for the first time that she was not the only blue-eyed, fair-haired, straight-nosed, slim-figured girl of between twenty-five and thirty years of age. London was evidently full of such girls, and forty or fifty of them at least were grouped outside No. 7 Endersleigh Street.

'Competition,' said Jane. 'I'd better join the queue quickly.'

She did so, just as three more girls turned the corner of the street. Others followed them. Jane amused herself by taking stock of her immediate neighbours. In each case she managed to find something wrong – fair eyelashes instead of dark, eyes more grey than blue, fair hair that owed its fairness to art and not to Nature, interesting variations in noses, and figures that only an all-embracing charity could have described as slim. Jane's spirits rose.

'I believe I've got as good an all-round chance as any one,' she murmured to herself. 'I wonder what it's all about? A beauty chorus, I hope.'

The queue was moving slowly but steadily forward. Presently a second stream of girls began issuing from inside the house. Some of them tossed their heads, some of them smirked.

'Rejected,' said Jane, with glee. 'I hope to goodness they won't be full up before I get in.'

And still the queue of girls moved forwards. There were anxious glances in tiny mirrors, and a frenzied powdering of noses. Lipsticks were brandished freely.

'I wish I had a smarter hat,' said Jane to herself sadly.

At last it was her turn. Inside the door of the house was a glass door at one side, with the legend, Messrs Cuthbertsons, inscribed on it. It was through this glass door that the applicants were passing one by one. Jane's turn came. She drew a deep breath and entered.

Inside was an outer office, obviously intended for clerks. At the end was another glass door. Jane was directed to pass through this, and did so. She found herself in a smaller room. There was a big desk in it, and behind the desk was a keen-eyed man of middle age with a thick rather foreign-looking moustache. His glance swept over Jane, then he pointed to a door on the left.

'Wait in there, please,' he said crisply.

Jane obeyed. The apartment she entered was already occupied. Five girls sat there, all very upright and all glaring at each other. It was clear to Jane that she had been included amongst the likely candidates, and her spirits rose. Nevertheless, she was forced to admit that these five girls were equally eligible with herself as far as the terms of the advertisement went.

The time passed. Streams of girls were evidently passing through the inner office. Most of them were dismissed through another door giving on the corridor, but every now and then a recruit arrived to swell the select assembly. At half-past six there were fourteen girls assembled there.

Jane heard a murmur of voices from the inner office, and then the foreign-looking gentleman, whom she had nicknamed in her mind 'the Colonel' owing to the military character of his moustaches, appeared in the doorway.

'I will see you ladies one at a time, if you please,' he announced. 'In the order in which you arrived, please.'

Jane was, of course, the sixth on the list. Twenty minutes elapsed before she was called in. 'The Colonel' was standing with his hands behind his back. He put her through a rapid catechism, tested her knowledge of French, and measured her height.

'It is possible, mademoiselle,' he said in French, 'that you may suit. I do not know. But it is possible.'

'What is this post, if I may ask?' said Jane bluntly.

He shrugged his shoulders.

'That I cannot tell you as yet. If you are chosen – then you shall know.'

'This seems very mysterious,' objected Jane. 'I couldn't

possibly take up anything without knowing all about it. Is it connected with the stage, may I ask?'

'The stage? Indeed, no.'

'Oh!' said Jane, rather taken aback.

He was looking at her keenly.

'You have intelligence, yes? And discretion?'

'I've quantities of intelligence and discretion,' said Jane calmly. 'What about the pay?'

'The pay will amount to two thousand pounds – for a fortnight's work.'

'Oh!' said Jane faintly.

She was too taken aback by the munificence of the sum named to recover all at once.

The Colonel resumed speaking.

'One other young lady I have already selected. You and she are equally suitable. There may be others I have not yet seen. I will give you instructions as to your further proceedings. You know Harridge's Hotel?'

Jane gasped. Who in England did not know Harridge's Hotel? That famous hostelry situated modestly in a by-street of Mayfair, where notabilities and royalties arrived and departed as a matter of course. Only this morning Jane had read of the arrival of the Grand Duchess Pauline of Ostrova. She had come over to open a big bazaar in aid of Russian refugees, and was, of course, staying at Harridge's.

'Yes,' said Jane, in answer to the Colonel's question.

'Very good. Go there. Ask for Count Streptitch. Send up your card – you have a card?'

Jane produced one. The Colonel took it from her and inscribed in the corner a minute P. He handed the card back to her.

'That ensures that the count will see you. He will understand that you come from me. The final decision lies with him – and another. If he considers you suitable, he will explain matters to you, and you can accept or decline his proposal. Is that satisfactory?'

'Perfectly satisfactory,' said Jane.

'So far,' she murmured to herself as she emerged into the street, 'I can't see the catch. And yet, there must be one. There's no such thing as money for nothing. It must be crime! There's nothing else left.'

Her spirits rose. In moderation Jane did not object to crime. The papers had been full lately of the exploits of various girl bandits. Jane had seriously thought of becoming one if all else failed.

She entered the exclusive portals of Harridge's with slight trepidation. More than ever, she wished that she had a new hat.

But she walked bravely up to the bureau and produced her card, and asked for Count Streptitch without a shade of hesitation in her manner. She fancied that the clerk looked at her rather curiously. He took the card, however, and gave it to a small page boy with some low-voiced instructions which Jane did not catch. Presently the page returned, and Jane was invited to accompany him. They went up in the lift and along a corridor to some big double doors where the page knocked. A moment later Jane found herself in a big room, facing a tall thin man with a fair beard, who was holding her card in a languid white hand.

'Miss Jane Cleveland,' he read slowly. 'I am Count Streptitch.'

His lips parted suddenly in what was presumably intended to be a smile, disclosing two rows of white even teeth. But no effect of merriment was obtained.

'I understand that you applied in answer to our advertisement,' continued the count. 'The good Colonel Kranin sent you on here.'

'He *was* a colonel,' thought Jane, pleased with her perspicacity, but she merely bowed her head.

'You will pardon me if I ask you a few questions?'

He did not wait for a reply, but proceeded to put Jane through a catechism very similar to that of Colonel Kranin.

Her replies seemed to satisfy him. He nodded his head once or twice.

'I will ask you now, mademoiselle, to walk to the door and back again slowly.'

'Perhaps they want me to be a mannequin,' thought Jane, as she complied. 'But they wouldn't pay two thousand pounds to a mannequin. Still, I suppose I'd better not ask questions yet awhile.'

Count Streptitch was frowning. He tapped on the table with his white fingers. Suddenly he rose, and opening the door of an adjoining room, he spoke to some one inside.

He returned to his seat, and a short middle-aged lady came through the door, closing it behind her. She was plump and extremely ugly, but had nevertheless the air of being a person of importance.

'Well, Anna Michaelovna,' said the count. 'What do you think of her?'

The lady looked Jane up and down much as though the girl had been a wax-work at a show. She made no pretence of any greeting.

'She might do,' she said at length. 'Of actual likeness in the real sense of the word, there is very little. But the figure and the colouring are very good, better than any of the others. What do you think of it, Feodor Alexandrovitch?'

'I agree with you, Anna Michaelovna.'

'Does she speak French?'

'Her French is excellent.'

Jane felt more and more of a dummy. Neither of these strange people appeared to remember that she was a human being.

'But will she be discreet?' asked the lady, frowning heavily at the girl.

'This is the Princess Poporensky,' said Count Streptitch to Jane in French. 'She asks whether you can be discreet?'

Jane addressed her reply to the princess.

'Until I have had the position explained to me, I can hardly make promises.'

'It is just what she says there, the little one,' remarked the lady. 'I think she is intelligent, Feodor Alexandrovitch – more intelligent than the others. Tell me, little one, have you also courage?'

'I don't know,' said Jane puzzled. 'I don't particularly like being hurt, but I can bear it.'

'Ah! that is not what I mean. You do not mind danger, no?'

'Oh!' said Jane. 'Danger! That's all right. I like danger.'

'And you are poor? You would like to earn much money?'

'Try me,' said Jane with something approaching enthusiasm.

Count Streptitch and Princess Poporensky exchanged glances. Then, simultaneously, they nodded.

'Shall I explain matters, Anna Michaelovna?' the former asked.

The princess shook her head.

'Her Highness wishes to do that herself.'

'It is unnecessary – and unwise.'

'Nevertheless those are her commands. I was to bring the girl in as soon as you had done with her.'

Streptitch shrugged his shoulders. Clearly he was not pleased. Equally clearly he had no intention of disobeying the edict. He turned to Jane.

'The Princess Poporensky will present you to Her Highness the Grand Duchess Pauline. Do not be alarmed.'

Jane was not in the least alarmed. She was delighted at the idea of being presented to a real live grand duchess. There was nothing of the Socialist about Jane. For the moment she had even ceased to worry about her hat.

The Princess Poporensky led the way, waddling along with a gait that she managed to invest with a certain dignity in spite of adverse circumstances. They passed through the adjoining room, which was a kind of ante-chamber, and the princess knocked upon a door in the farther wall. A voice from inside replied and the Princess opened the door and passed in, Jane close upon her heels.

'Let me present to you, madame,' said the princess in a solemn voice, 'Miss Jane Cleveland.'

A young woman who had been sitting in a big arm-chair at the other end of the room jumped up and ran forward. She stared fixedly at Jane for a minute or two, and then laughed merrily.

'But this is splendid, Anna,' she cried. 'I never imagined we should succeed so well. Come, let us see ourselves side by side.

Taking Jane's arm, she drew the girl across the room, pausing before a full-length mirror which hung on the wall.

'You see?' she cried delightedly. 'It is a perfect match?'

Already, with her first glance at the Grand Duchess Pauline, Jane had begun to understand. The Grand Duchess was a young woman perhaps a year or two older than Jane. She had the same shade of fair hair, and the same slim figure. She was, perhaps, a shade taller. Now that they stood side by side, the likeness was very apparent. Detail for detail, the colouring was almost exactly the same.

The Grand Duchess clapped her hands. She seemed an extremely cheerful young woman.

'Nothing could be better,' she declared. 'You must congratulate Feodor Alexandrovitch for me, Anna. He has indeed done well.'

'As yet, madame,' murmured the princess, in a low voice, 'this young woman does not know what is required of her.'

'True,' said the Grand Duchess, becoming somewhat calmer in manner. 'I forgot. Well, I will enlighten her. Leave us together, Anna Michaelovna.'

'But, madame——'

'Leave us alone, I say.'

She stamped her foot angrily. With considerable reluctance Anna Michaelovna left the room. The Grand Duchess sat down and motioned to Jane to do the same.

'They are tiresome, these old women,' remarked Pauline. 'But one has to have them. Anna Michaelovna is better than most. Now then, Miss – ah, yes, Miss Jane Cleveland. I like the name. I like you too. You are sympathetic. I can tell at once if people are sympathetic.'

'That's very clever of you, ma'am,' said Jane, speaking for the first time.

'I am clever,' said Pauline calmly. 'Come now, I will explain things to you. Not that there is much to explain. You know the history of Ostrova. Practically all of my family are dead – massacred by the Communists. I am, perhaps, the last of my line. I am a woman, I cannot sit upon the throne. You think they would let me be. But no, wherever I go attempts are made to assassinate me. Absurd, is it not? These vodka-soaked brutes never have any sense of proportion.'

'I see,' said Jane, feeling that something was required of her.

'For the most part I live in retirement – where I can take precautions, but now and then I have to take part in public ceremonies. While I am here, for instance, I have to attend several semi-public functions. Also in Paris on my way back. I have an estate in Hungary, you know. The sport there is magnificent.'

'Is it really?' said Jane.

'Superb. I adore sport. Also – I ought not to tell you this, but I shall because your face is so sympathetic – there are plans being made there – very quietly, you understand. Altogether it is very important that I should not be assassinated during the next two weeks.'

'But surely the police——' began Jane.

'The police? Oh, yes, they are very good, I believe. And we too – we have our spies. It is possible that I shall be forewarned when the attempt is to take place. But then, again, I might not.'

She shrugged her shoulders.

'I begin to understand,' said Jane slowly. 'You want me to take your place?'

'Only on certain occasions,' said the Grand Duchess eagerly. 'You must be somewhere at hand, you understand? I may require you twice, three times, four times in the next fortnight. Each time it will be upon the occasion of some public function. Naturally in intimacy of any kind, you could not represent me.'

'Of course not,' agreed Jane.

'You will do very well indeed. It was clever of Feodor Alexandrovitch to think of an advertisement, was it not?'

'Supposing,' said Jane, 'that I get assassinated?'

The Grand Duchess shrugged her shoulders.

'There is the risk, of course, but according to our own secret information, they want to kidnap me, not kill me outright. But I will be quite honest – it is always possible that they might throw a bomb.'

'I see,' said Jane.

She tried to imitate the light-hearted manner of Pauline. She wanted very much to come to the question of money, but did not quite see how best to introduce the subject. But Pauline saved her the trouble.

'We will pay you well, of course,' she said carelessly. 'I cannot remember now exactly how much Feodor Alexandrovitch suggested. We were speaking in francs or kronen.'

'Colonel Kranin,' said Jane, 'said something about two thousand pounds.'

'That was it,' said Pauline, brightening. 'I remember now. It is enough, I hope? Or would you rather have three thousand?'

'Well,' said Jane, 'if it's all the same to you, I'd rather have three thousand.'

'You are business-like, I see,' said the Grand Duchess kindly. 'I wish I was. But I have no idea of money at all. What I want I have to have, that is all.'

It seemed to Jane a simple but admirable attitude of mind.

'And of course, as you say, there is danger,' Pauline continued thoughtfully. 'Although you do not look to me as though you minded danger. I do not myself. I hope you do not think that it is because I am a coward that I want you to take my place? You see, it is most important for Ostrova that I should marry and have at least two sons. After that, it does not matter what happens to me.'

'I see,' said Jane.

'And you accept?'

'Yes,' said Jane resolutely. 'I accept.'

Pauline clapped her hands vehemently several times. Princess Poporensky appeared immediately.

'I have told her all, Anna,' announced the Grand Duchess. 'She will do what we want, and she is to have three thousand pounds. Tell Feodor to make a note of it. She is really very like me, is she not? I think she is better looking, though.'

The princess waddled out of the room, and returned with Count Streptitch.

'We have arranged everything, Feodor Alexandrovitch,' the Grand Duchess said.

He bowed.

'Can she play her part, I wonder?' he queried, eyeing Jane doubtfully.

'I'll show you,' said the girl suddenly. 'You permit, ma'am?' she said to the Grand Duchess.

The latter nodded delightedly.

Jane stood up.

'But this is splendid, Anna,' she said. 'I never imagined we should succeed so well. Come, let us see ourselves, side by side.'

And, as Pauline had done, she drew the other girl to the glass.

'You see? A perfect match!'

Words, manner and gesture, it was an excellent imitation

of Pauline's greeting. The princess nodded her head, and uttered a grunt of approbation.

'It is good, that,' she declared. 'It would deceive most people.'

'You are very clever,' said Pauline appreciatively. 'I could not imitate any one else to save my life.'

Jane believed her. It had already struck her that Pauline was a young woman who was very much herself.

'Anna will arrange details with you,' said the Grand Duchess. 'Take her into my bedroom, Anna, and try some of my clothes on her.'

She nodded a gracious farewell, and Jane was convoyed away by the Princess Poporensky.

'This is what Her Highness will wear to open the bazaar,' explained the old lady, holding up a daring creation of white and black. 'That is in three days time. It may be necessary for you to take her place there. We do not know. We have not yet received information.'

At Anna's bidding, Jane slipped off her own shabby garments, and tried on the frock. It fitted her perfectly. The other nodded approvingly.

'It is almost perfect – just a shade long on you, because you are an inch or so shorter than Her Highness.'

'That is easily remedied,' said Jane quickly. 'The Grand Duchess wears low-heeled shoes, I noticed. If I wear the same kind of shoes, but with high heels, it will adjust things nicely.'

Anna Michaelovna showed her the shoes that the Grand Duchess usually wore with the dress. Lizard skin with a strap across. Jane memorized them, and arranged to get a pair just like them, but with different heels.

'It would be well,' said Anna Michaelovna, 'for you to have a dress of distinctive colour and material quite unlike Her Highness's. Then in case it becomes necessary for you to change places at a moment's notice, the substitution is less likely to be noticed.'

Jane thought a minute.

'What about flame red marocain? And I might, perhaps, have plain glass pince-nez. That alters the appearance very much.'

Both suggestions were approved, and they went into further details.

Jane left the hotel with bank-notes for a hundred pounds in her purse, and instructions to purchase the necessary outfit and engage rooms at the Blitz Hotel as Miss Montresor of New York.

On the second day after this, Count Streptitch called upon her there.

'A transformation indeed,' he said, as he bowed.

Jane made him a mock bow in return. She was enjoying the new clothes and the luxury of her life very much.

'All this is very nice,' she sighed. 'But I suppose that your visit means I must get busy and earn my money.'

'That is so. We have received information. It seems possible that an attempt will be made to kidnap Her Highness on the way home from the bazaar. That is to take place, as you know, at Orion House, which is about ten miles out of London. Her Highness will be forced to attend the bazaar in person, as the Countess of Anchester, who is promoting it, knows her personally. But the following is the plan I have concocted.'

Jane listened attentively as he outlined it to her.

She asked a few questions, and finally declared that she understood perfectly the part that she had to play.

The next day dawned bright and clear – a perfect day for one of the great events of the London Season, the bazaar at Orion House, promoted by the Countess of Anchester in aid of Ostrovian refugees in this country.

Having regard to the uncertainty of the English climate, the bazaar itself took place within the spacious rooms of Orion House, which has been for five hundred years in the possession of the Earls of Anchester. Various collections had been loaned, and a charming idea was the gift by a hundred society women of one pearl each taken from their own necklaces, each pearl to be sold by auction on the second day. There were also numerous side-shows and attractions in the grounds.

Jane was there early in the rôle of Miss Montresor. She wore a dress of flame-coloured marocain, and a small red cloche hat. On her feet were high-heeled lizard-skin shoes.

The arrival of the Grand Duchess Pauline was a great event. She was escorted to the platform and duly presented with a bouquet of roses by a small child. She made a short but charming speech and declared the bazaar open. Count Streptitch and Princess Poporensky were in attendance upon her.

She wore the dress that Jane had seen, white with a bold design of black, and her hat was a small cloche of black with a profusion of white ospreys hanging over the brim and a tiny lace veil coming half-way down the face. Jane smiled to herself.

The Grand Duchess went round the bazaar, visiting every stall, making a few purchases, and being uniformly gracious. Then she prepared to depart.

Jane was prompt to take up her cue. She requested a word with the Princess Poporensky and asked to be presented to the Grand Duchess.

'Ah, yes!' said Pauline, in a clear voice. 'Miss Montresor, I remember the name. She is an American journalist, I believe. She has done much for our cause. I should be glad to give her a short interview for her paper. Is there anywhere where we could be undisturbed?'

A small anteroom was immediately placed at the Grand Duchess's disposal, and Count Streptitch was despatched to bring in Miss Montresor. As soon as he had done so, and withdrawn again, the Princess Poporensky remaining in attendance, a rapid exchange of garments took place.

Three minutes later, the door opened and the Grand

Duchess emerged, her bouquet of roses held up to her face.

Bowing graciously, and uttering a few words of farewell to Lady Anchester in French, she passed out and entered her car which was waiting. Princess Poporensky took her place beside her, and the car drove off.

'Well,' said Jane, 'that's that. I wonder how Miss Montresor's getting on.'

'No one will notice her. She can slip out quietly.'

'That's true,' said Jane. 'I did it nicely, didn't I?'

'You acted your part with great discretion.'

'Why isn't the count with us?'

'He was forced to remain. Some one must watch over the safety of Her Highness.'

'I hope nobody's going to throw bombs,' said Jane apprehensively. 'Hi! we're turning off the main road. Why's that?'

Gathering speed, the car was shooting down a side road.

Jane jumped up and put her head out of the window, remonstrating with the driver. He only laughed and increased his speed. Jane sank back into her seat again.

'Your spies were right,' she said, with a laugh. 'We're for it all right. I suppose the longer I keep it up, the safer it is for the Grand Duchess. At all events we must give her time to return to London safely.'

At the prospect of danger, Jane's spirits rose. She had not relished the prospect of a bomb, but this type of adventure appealed to her sporting instincts.

Suddenly, with a grinding of brakes, the car pulled up in its own length. A man jumped on the step. In his hand was a revolver.

'Put your hands up,' he snarled.

The Princess Poporensky's hands rose swiftly, but Jane merely looked at him disdainfully, and kept her hands on her lap.

'Ask him the meaning of this outrage,' she said in French to her companion.

But before the latter had time to say a word, the man broke in. He poured out a torrent of words in some foreign language.

Not understanding a single thing, Jane merely shrugged her shoulders and said nothing. The chauffeur had got down from his seat and joined the other man.

'Will the illustrious lady be pleased to descend?' he asked, with a grin.

Raising the flowers to her face again, Jane stepped out of the car. The Princess Poporensky followed her.

'Will the illustrious lady come this way?'

Jane took no notice of the man's mock insolent manner, but of her own accord she walked towards a low-built, rambling house which stood about a hundred yards away from where the car had stopped. The road had been a *cul-de-sac* ending in the gateway and drive which led to this apparently untenanted building.

The man, still brandishing his pistol, came close behind the two women. As they passed up the steps, he brushed past them and flung open a door on the left. It was an empty room, into which a table and two chairs had evidently been brought.

Jane passed in and sat down. Anna Michaelovna followed her. The man banged the door and turned the key.

Jane walked to the window and looked out.

'I could jump out, of course,' she remarked. 'But I shouldn't get far. No, we'll just have to stay here for the present and make the best of it. I wonder if they'll bring us anything to eat?'

About half an hour later her question was answered.

A big bowl of steaming soup was brought in and placed on the table in front of her. Also two pieces of dry bread.

'No luxury for aristocrats evidently,' remarked Jane cheerily as the door was shut and locked again. 'Will you start, or shall I?'

The Princess Poporensky waved the mere idea of food aside with horror.

'How could I eat? Who knows what danger my mistress might not be in?'

'She's all right,' said Jane. 'It's myself I'm worrying about. You know these people won't be at all pleased when they find they have got hold of the wrong person. In fact, they may be very unpleasant. I shall keep up the haughty Grand Duchess stunt as long as I can, and do a bunk if the opportunity offers.'

The Princess Poporensky offered no reply.

Jane, who was hungry, drank up all the soup. It had a curious taste, but was hot and savoury.

Afterwards she felt rather sleepy. The Princess Poporensky seemed to be weeping quietly. Jane arranged herself on her uncomfortable chair in the least uncomfortable way, and allowed her head to droop.

She slept.

Jane awoke with a start. She had an idea that she had been a very long time asleep. Her head felt heavy and uncomfortable.

And then suddenly she saw something that jerked her faculties wide awake again.

She was wearing the flame-coloured marocain frock.

She sat up and looked around her. Yes, she was still in the room in the empty house. Everything was exactly as it had been when she went to sleep, except for two facts. The first fact was that the Princess Poporensky was no longer sitting on the other chair. The second was her own inexplicable change of costume.

'I can't have dreamt it,' said Jane. 'Because if I'd dreamt it, I shouldn't be here.'

She looked across at the window and registered a second significant fact. When she had gone to sleep the sun had been pouring through the window. Now the house threw a sharp shadow on the sunlit drive.

'The house faces west,' she reflected. 'It was afternoon

when I went to sleep. Therefore it must be tomorrow morning now. Therefore that soup was drugged. Therefore – oh, I don't know. It all seems mad.'

She got up and went to the door. It was unlocked. She explored the house. It was silent and empty.

Jane put her hand to her aching head and tried to think.

And then she caught sight of a torn newspaper lying by the front door. It had glaring headlines which caught her eye.

'American Girl Bandit in England,' she read. 'The Girl in the Red Dress. Sensational hold-up at Orion House Bazaar.'

Jane staggered out into the sunlight. Sitting on the steps she read, her eyes growing bigger and bigger. The facts were short and succinct.

Just after the departure of the Grand Duchess Pauline, three men and a girl in a red dress had produced revolvers and successfully held up the crowd. They had annexed the hundred pearls and made a getaway in a fast racing car. Up to now, they had not been traced.

In the stop press (it was a late evening paper) were a few words to the effect that the 'girl bandit in the red dress' had been staying at the Blitz as a Miss Montresor of New York.

'I'm dished,' said Jane. 'Absolutely dished. I always knew there was a catch in it.'

And then she started. A strange sound had smote the air. The voice of a man, uttering one word at frequent intervals.

'Damn,' it said. 'Damn.' And yet again, 'Damn!'

Jane thrilled to the sound. It expressed so exactly her own feelings. She ran down the steps. By the corner of them lay a young man. He was endeavouring to raise his head from the ground. His face struck Jane as one of the nicest faces she had ever seen. It was freckled and slightly quizzical in expression.

'Damn my head,' said the young man. 'Damn it. I——'

He broke off and stared at Jane.

'I must be dreaming,' he said faintly.

'That's what I said,' said Jane. 'But we're not. What's the matter with your head?'

'Somebody hit me on it. Fortunately it's a thick one.'

He pulled himself into a sitting position, and made a wry face.

'My brain will begin to function shortly, I expect. I'm still in the same old spot, I see.'

'How did you get here?' asked Jane curiously.

'That's a long story. By the way, you're not the Grand Duchess What's-her-name, are you?'

'I'm not. I'm plain Jane Cleveland.'

'You're not plain, anyway,' said the young man, looking at her with frank admiration.

Jane blushed.

'I ought to get you some water or something, oughtn't I?' she asked uncertainly.

'I believe it is customary,' agreed the young man. 'All the same, I'd rather have whisky if you can find it.'

Jane was unable to find any whisky. The young man took a deep draught of water, and announced himself better.

'Shall I relate my adventures, or will you relate yours?' he asked.

'You first.'

'There's nothing much to mine. I happened to notice that the Grand Duchess went into that room with low-heeled shoes on and came out with high-heeled ones. It struck me as rather odd. I don't like things to be odd.

'I followed the car on my motor bicycle, I saw you taken into the house. About ten minutes later a big racing car came tearing up. A girl in red got out and three men. She had low-heeled shoes on, all right. They went into the house. Presently low heels came out dressed in black and white, and went off in the first car, with an old pussy and a tall man with a fair beard. The others went off in the racing car. I thought they'd all gone, and was just trying to get in at that window and rescue you when some one hit me on the head from behind. That's all. Now for your turn.'

Jane related her adventures.

'And it's awfully lucky for me that you did follow,' she ended. 'Do you see what an awful hole I should have been in otherwise. The Grand Duchess would have had a perfect alibi. She left the bazaar before the hold up began, and arrived in London in her car. Would anybody ever have believed my fantastic improbable story?'

'Not on your life,' said the young man with conviction.

They had been so absorbed in their respective narratives that they had been quite oblivious of their surroundings. They looked up now with a slight start to see a tall sad-faced man leaning against the house. He nodded at them.

'Very interesting,' he commented.

'Who are you?' demanded Jane.

The sad-faced man's eyes twinkled a little.

'Detective-Inspector Farrell,' he said gently. 'I've been very interested in hearing your story and this young lady's. We might have found a little difficulty in believing hers, but for one or two things.'

'For instance?'

'Well, you see, we heard this morning that the real Grand Duchess had eloped with a chauffeur in Paris.'

Jane gasped.

'And then we knew that this American "girl bandit" had come to this country, and we expected a coup of some kind. We'll have laid hands on them very soon, I can promise you that. Excuse me a minute, will you?'

He ran up the steps into the house.

'Well!' said Jane. She put a lot of force into the expression.

'I think it was awfully clever of you to notice those shoes,' she said suddenly.

'Not at all,' said the young man. 'I was brought up in the boot trade. My father's a sort of boot king. He wanted me to go into the trade – marry and settle down. All that sort of thing. Nobody in particular – just the principle of the thing. But I wanted to be an artist.' He sighed.

'I'm so sorry,' said Jane kindly.

'I've been trying for six years. There's no blinking it. I'm a rotten painter. I've a good mind to chuck it and go home like the prodigal son. There's a good billet waiting for me.'

'A job is the great thing,' agreed Jane wistfully. 'Do you think you could get me one trying on boots somewhere?'

'I could give you a better one that that – if you'd take it.

'Oh, what?'

'Never mind now. I'll tell you later. You know, until yesterday I never saw a girl I felt I could marry.'

'Yesterday?'

'At the bazaar. And then I saw her – the one and only Her!'

He looked very hard at Jane.

'How beautiful the delphiniums are,' said Jane hurriedly, with very pink cheeks.

'They're lupins,' said the young man.

'It doesn't matter,' said Jane.

'Not a bit,' he agreed. And he drew a little nearer.

In a Glass Darkly

I've no explanation of this story. I've no theories about the why and wherefore of it. It's just a thing – that happened.

All the same, I sometimes wonder how things would have gone if I'd noticed at the time just that one essential detail that I never appreciated until so many years afterwards. If I *had* noticed it – well, I suppose the course of three lives would have been entirely altered. Somehow – that's a very frightening thought.

For the beginning of it all, I've got to go back to the summer of 1914 – just before the war – when I went back to Badgeworthy with Neil Carslake. Neil was, I suppose, about my best friend. I'd known his brother Alan too, but not so well. Sylvia, their sister, I'd never met. She was two years younger than Alan and three years younger than Neil. Twice, while we were at school together, I'd been going to spend part of the holidays with Neil at Badgeworthy and twice something had intervened. So it came about that I was twenty-three when I first saw Neil and Alan's home.

We were to be quite a big party there. Neil's sister Sylvia had just got engaged to a fellow called Charles Crawley. He was, so Neil said, a good deal older than she was, but a thoroughly decent chap and quite reasonably well-off.

We arrived, I remember, about seven o'clock in the

evening. Everyone had gone to his room to dress for dinner. Neil took me to mine. Badgeworthy was an attractive, rambling old house. It had been added to freely in the last three centuries and was full of little steps up and down, and unexpected staircases. It was the sort of house in which it's not too easy to find your way about. I remember Neil promised to come and fetch me on his way down to dinner. I was feeling a little shy at the prospect of meeting his people for the first time. I remember saying with a laugh that it was the kind of house where one expected to meet ghosts in the passages, and he said carelessly that he believed the place was said to be haunted but that none of them had ever seen anything, and he didn't even know what form the ghost was supposed to take.

Then he hurried away and I set to work to dive into my suitcases for my evening clothes. The Carslakes weren't well-off; they clung on to their old home, but there were no menservants to unpack for you or valet you.

Well, I'd just got to the stage of tying my tie. I was standing in front of the glass. I could see my own face and shoulders and behind them the wall of the room – a plain stretch of wall just broken in the middle by a door – and just as I had finally settled my tie I noticed that the door was opening.

I don't know why I didn't turn round – I think that would have been the natural thing to do; anyway, I didn't. I just watched the door swing slowly open – and as it swung I saw into the room beyond.

It was a bedroom – a larger room than mine – with two bedsteads in it, and suddenly I caught my breath.

For at the foot of one of those beds was a girl and round her neck were a pair of man's hands and the man was slowly forcing her backwards and squeezing her throat as he did so, so that the girl was being slowly suffocated.

There wasn't the least possibility of a mistake. What I saw was perfectly clear. What was being done was murder.

I could see the girl's face clearly, her vivid golden hair, the agonized terror of her beautiful face, slowly suffusing with blood. Of the man I could only see his back, his hands, and a scar that ran down the left side of his face towards his neck.

It's taken some time to tell, but in reality only a moment or two passed while I stared dumbfounded. Then I wheeled round to the rescue . . .

And on the wall behind me, the wall reflected in the glass, there was only a large Victorian mahogany wardrobe. No open door – no scene of violence. I swung back to the mirror. The mirror reflected only the wardrobe . . .

I passed my hands across my eyes. Then I sprang across the room and tried to pull forward the wardrobe and at that moment Neil entered by the other door from the passage and asked me what the hell I was trying to do.

He must have thought me slightly barmy as I turned on him and demanded whether there was a door behind the wardrobe. He said, yes, there was a door, it led into the next room. I asked him who was occupying the room and he said people called Oldham – a Major Oldham and his wife. I asked him then if Mrs Oldham had very fair hair and when he replied dryly that she was dark I began to realize that I was probably making a fool of myself. I pulled myself together, made some lame explanation and we went downstairs together. I told myself that I must have had some kind of hallucination – and felt generally rather ashamed and a bit of an ass.

And then – and then – Neil said, 'My sister Sylvia,' and I was looking into the lovely face of the girl I had just seen being suffocated to death . . . and I was introduced to her fiancé, a tall dark man *with a scar down the left side of his face*.

Well – that's that. I'd like you to think and say what you'd have done in my place. Here was the girl – the identical girl – and here was the man I'd seen throttling her – and they were to be married in about a month's time . . .

Had I – or had I not – had a prophetic vision of the future? Would Sylvia and her husband come down here to stay some time in the future, and be given that room (the best spare room) and would that scene I'd witnessed take place in grim reality?

What was I to do about it? *Could* I do anything? Would anyone – Neil – or the girl herself – would they believe me?

I turned the whole business over and over in my mind the week I was down there. To speak or not to speak? And almost at once another complication set in. You see, I fell in love with Sylvia Carslake the first moment I saw her . . . I wanted her more than anything on earth . . . And in a way that tied my hands.

And yet, if I didn't say anything, Sylvia would marry Charles Crawley and Crawley would kill her . . .

And so, the day before I left, I blurted it all out to her. I said I expected she'd think me touched in the intellect or something, but I swore solemnly that I'd seen the thing just as I told it to her and that I felt if she was determined to marry Crawley, I ought to tell her my strange experience.

She listened very quietly. There was something in her eyes I didn't understand. She wasn't angry at all. When I'd finished, she just thanked me gravely. I kept repeating like an idiot, 'I *did* see it. I really did see it,' and she said, 'I'm sure you did if you say so. I believe you.'

Well, the upshot was that I went off not knowing whether I'd done right or been a fool, and a week later Sylvia broke off her engagement to Charles Crawley.

After that the war happened, and there wasn't much leisure for thinking of anything else. Once or twice when I was on leave, I came across Sylvia, but as far as possible I avoided her.

I loved her and wanted her just as badly as ever, but I felt somehow that it wouldn't be playing the game. It was owing to me that she'd broken off her engagement to Crawley, and I kept saying to myself that I could only justify the action I had taken by making my attitude a purely disinterested one.

Then, in 1916, Neil was killed and it fell to me to tell Sylvia about his last moments. We couldn't remain on a formal footing after that. Sylvia had adored Neil and he had been my best friend. She was sweet – adorably sweet in her grief. I just managed to hold my tongue and went out again praying that a bullet might end the whole miserable business. Life without Sylvia wasn't worth living.

But there was no bullet with my name on it. One nearly got me below the right ear and was deflected by a cigarette case in my pocket, but I came through unscathed. Charles Crawley was killed in action at the beginning of 1918.

Somehow – that made a difference. I came home in the autumn of 1918 just before the Armistice and I went straight to Sylvia and told her that I loved her. I hadn't much hope that she'd care for me straight away, and you could have knocked me down with a feather when she asked me why I hadn't told her sooner. I stammered out something about Crawley and she said, 'But why did you think I broke it off with him?' And then she told me that she'd fallen in love with me just as I'd done with her – from the very first minute.

I said I thought she'd broken off her engagement because of the story I told her and she laughed scornfully and said that if you loved a man you wouldn't be as cowardly as that, and we went over that old vision of mine again and agreed that it was queer, but nothing more.

Well, there's nothing much to tell for some time after that. Sylvia and I were married and we were happy. But I realized, as soon as she was really mine, that I wasn't cut out for the best kind of husband. I loved Sylvia devotedly, but I was jealous, absurdly jealous of anyone she so much as smiled at. It amused her at first. I think she even rather liked it. It proved, at least, how devoted I was.

As for me, I realized quite fully and unmistakably that I was not only making a fool of myself, but that I was endangering all the peace and happiness of our life together. I knew, I say, but I couldn't change. Every time Sylvia got a letter she didn't show to me I wondered who it was from. If she laughed and talked with any man, I found myself getting sulky and watchful.

At first, as I say, Sylvia laughed at me. She thought it a huge joke. Then she didn't think the joke so funny. Finally she didn't think it a joke at all –

And slowly, she began to draw away from me. Not in any physical sense, but she withdrew her secret mind from me. I no longer knew what her thoughts were. She was kind – but sadly, as though from a long distance.

Little by little I realized that she no longer loved me. Her love had died and it was I who had killed it . . .

The next step was inevitable. I found myself waiting for it – dreading it . . .

Then Derek Wainwright came into our lives. He had everything that I hadn't. He had brains and a witty tongue. He was good-looking, too, and – I'm forced to admit it – a thoroughly good chap. As soon as I saw him I said to myself, 'This is just the man for Sylvia . . .'

She fought against it. I know she struggled . . . but I gave her no help. I couldn't. I was entrenched in my gloomy, sullen reserve. I was suffering like hell – and I couldn't stretch out a finger to save myself. I didn't help her. I made things worse. I let loose at her one day – a string of savage, unwarranted abuse. I was nearly mad with jealousy and misery. The things I said were cruel and untrue and I knew while I was saying them how cruel and how untrue they were. And yet I took a savage pleasure in saying them . . .

I remember how Sylvia flushed and shrank . . .

I drove her to the edge of endurance.

I remember she said, 'This can't go on . . .'

When I came home that night the house was empty – empty. There was a note – quite in the traditional fashion.

In it she said that she was leaving me – for good. She was

going down to Badgeworthy for a day or two. After that she was going to the one person who loved her and needed her. I was to take that as final.

I suppose that up to then I hadn't really believed my own suspicions. This confirmation in black and white of my worst fears sent me raving mad. I went down to Badgeworthy after her as fast as the car would take me.

She had just changed her frock for dinner, I remember, when I burst into the room. I can see her face – startled – beautiful – afraid.

I said, 'No one but me shall ever have you. No one.'

And I caught her throat in my hands and gripped it and bent her backwards.

And suddenly I saw our reflection in the mirror. Sylvia choking and myself strangling her, and the scar on my cheek where the bullet grazed it under the right ear.

No – I didn't kill her. That sudden revelation paralyzed me and I loosed my grip and let her slip on to the floor . . .

And then I broke down – and she comforted me . . . Yes, she comforted me.

I told her everything and she told me that by the phrase 'the person who loved and needed her' she had meant her brother Alan . . . We saw into each other's hearts that night, and I don't think, from that moment, that we ever drifted away from each other again . . .

It's a sobering thought to go through life with – that, but for the grace of God and a mirror, one might be a murderer . . .

One thing did die that night – the devil of jealousy that had possessed me so long . . .

But I wonder sometimes – suppose I hadn't made that initial mistake – the scar on the *left* cheek – when really it was the *right* – reversed by the mirror . . . Should I have been so sure the man was Charles Crawley? Would I have warned Sylvia? Would she be married to me – or to him?

Or are the past and future all one?

I'm a simple fellow – and I can't pretend to understand these things – but I saw what I saw – and because of what I saw, Sylvia and I are together in the old-fashioned words – till death do us part. And perhaps beyond . . .

The Case of the Middle-aged Wife

Four grunts, an indignant voice asking why nobody could leave a hat alone, a slammed door, and Mr Packington had departed to catch the eight-forty-five to the city. Mrs Packington sat on at the breakfast table. Her face was flushed, her lips were pursed, and the only reason she was not crying was that at the last minute anger had taken the place of grief. 'I won't stand it,' said Mrs Packington. 'I won't stand it!' She remained for some moments brooding, and then murmured: 'The minx. Nasty sly little cat! How George can be such a fool!'

Anger faded; grief came back. Tears came into Mrs Packington's eyes and rolled slowly down her middle-aged cheeks. 'It's all very well to say I won't stand it, but what can I do?'

Suddenly she felt alone, helpless, utterly forlorn. Slowly she took up the morning paper and read, not for the first time, an advertisement on the front page.

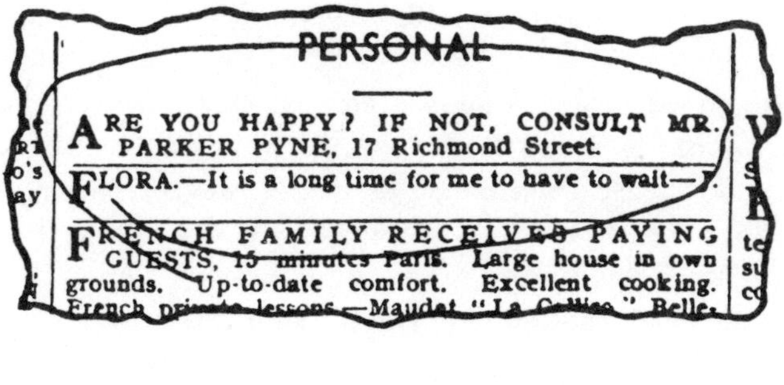
PERSONAL

ARE YOU HAPPY? IF NOT, CONSULT MR. PARKER PYNE, 17 Richmond Street.

FLORA.—It is a long time for me to have to wait—F.

FRENCH FAMILY RECEIVES PAYING GUESTS, 15 minutes Paris. Large house in own grounds. Up-to-date comfort. Excellent cooking.

'Absurd!' said Mrs Packington. 'Utterly absurd.' Then: 'After all, I might just see . . .'

Which explains why at eleven o'clock Mrs Packington, a little nervous, was being shown into Mr Parker Pyne's private office.

As has been said, Mrs Packington was nervous, but somehow or other, the mere sight of Mr Parker Pyne brought a feeling of reassurance. He was large, not to say fat; he had a bald head of noble proportions, strong glasses, and little twinkling eyes.

'Pray sit down,' said Mr Parker Pyne. 'You have come in answer to my advertisement?' he added helpfully.

'Yes,' said Mrs Packington, and stopped there.

'And you are not happy,' said Mr Parker Pyne in a cheerful, matter-of-fact voice. 'Very few people are. You would really be surprised if you knew how few people are happy.'

'Indeed?' said Mrs Packington, not feeling, however, that it mattered where other people were unhappy or not.

'Not interesting to you, I know,' said Mr Parker Pyne, 'but very interesting to *me*. You see, for thirty-five years of my life I have been engaged in the compiling of statistics in a government office. Now I have retired, and it has occurred to me to use the experience I have gained in a novel fashion. It is all so simple. Unhappiness can be classified under five main heads – no more, I assure you. Once you know the cause of a malady, the remedy should not be impossible.

'I stand in the place of the doctor. The doctor first diagnoses the patient's disorder, then he proceeds to recommend a course of treatment. There are cases where no treatment can be of any avail. If that is so, I say frankly that I can do nothing. But I assure you, Mrs Packington, that if I undertake a case, the cure is practically guaranteed.'

Could it be so? Was this nonsense, or could it, perhaps, be true? Mrs Packington gazed at him hopefully.

'Shall we diagnose your case?' said Mr Parker Pyne,

smiling. He leaned back in his chair and brought the tips of his fingers together. 'The trouble concerns your husband. You have had, on the whole, a happy married life. Your husband has, I think, prospered. I think there is a young lady concerned in the case – perhaps a young lady in your husband's office.'

'A typist,' said Mrs Packington. 'A nasty made-up little minx, all lipstick and silk stockings and curls.' The words rushed from her.

Mr Parker Pyne nodded in a soothing manner. 'There is no real harm in it – that is your husband's phrase, I have no doubt.'

'His very words.'

'Why, therefore, should he not enjoy a pure friendship with this young lady, and be able to bring a little brightness, a little pleasure, into her dull existence? Poor child, she has so little fun. Those, I imagine, are his sentiments.'

Mrs Packington nodded with vigour. 'Humbug – all humbug! He takes her on the river – I'm fond of going on the river myself, but five or six years ago he said it interfered with his golf. But he can give up golf for *her*. I like the theatre – George has always said he's too tired to go out at night. Now he takes her out to dance – *dance*! And comes back at three in the morning. I – I——'

'And doubtless he deplores the fact that women are so jealous, so unreasonably jealous when there is absolutely no cause for jealousy?'

Again Mrs Pickington nodded. 'That's it.' She asked sharply: 'How do you know all this?'

'Statistics,' Mr Parker Pyne said simply.

'I'm so miserable,' said Mrs Packington. 'I've always been a good wife to George. I worked my fingers to the bone in our early days. I helped him to get on. I've never looked at any other man. His things are always mended, he gets good meals, and the house is well and economically run. And now that we've got on in the world and could enjoy ourselves and go about a bit and do all the things I've looked forward to doing some day – well, this!' She swallowed hard.

Mr Parker Pyne nodded gravely. 'I assure you I understand your case perfectly.'

'And – can you do anything?' She asked it almost in a whisper.

'Certainly, my dear lady. There is a cure. Oh, yes, there is a cure.'

'What is it?' She waited, round-eyed and expectant.

Mr Parker Pyne spoke quietly and firmly. 'You will place yourself in my hands, and the fee will be two hundred guineas.'

'Two hundred guineas!'

'Exactly. You can afford to pay such a fee, Mrs Packington. You would pay that sum for an operation. Happiness is just as important as bodily health.'

'I pay you afterwards, I suppose?'

'On the contrary,' said Mr Paarker Pyne. 'You pay in advance.'

Mrs Packington rose. 'I'm afraid I don't see my way——'

'To buying a pig in a poke?' said Mr Parker Pyne cheerfully. 'Well, perhaps you're right. It's a lot of money to risk. You've got to trust me, you see. You've got to pay the money and take a chance. Those are my terms.'

'Two hundred guineas!'

'Exactly. Two hundred guineas. It's a lot of money. Good morning, Mrs Packington. Let me know if you change your mind.' He shook hands with her, smiling in an unperturbed fashion.

When she had gone he pressed a buzzer on his desk. A forbidding-looking young woman with spectacles answered it.

'A file, please, Miss Lemon. And you might tell Claude that I am likely to want him shortly.'

'A new client?'

'A new client. At the moment she has jibbed, but she will

come back. Probably this afternoon about four. Enter her.'

'Schedule A?'

'Schedule A, of course. Interesting how every one thinks his own case unique. Well, well, warn Claude. Not too exotic, tell him. No scent and he'd better get his hair cut short.'

It was a quarter-past four when Mrs Packington once more entered Mr Parker Pyne's office. She drew out a cheque book, made out a cheque and passed it to him. A receipt was given.

'And now?' Mrs Packington looked at him hopefully.

'And now,' said Mr Parker Pyne, smiling, 'you will return home. By the first post tomorrow you will receive certain instructions which I shall be glad if you will carry out.'

Mrs Packington went home in a state of pleasant anticipation. Mr Packington came home in a defensive mood, ready to argue his position if the scene at the breakfast table was reopened. He was relieved, however, to find that his wife did not seem to be in a combative mood. She was unusually thoughtful.

George listened to the radio and wondered whether that dear child Nancy would allow him to give her a fur coat. She was very proud, he knew. He didn't want to offend her. Still, she had complained of the cold. That tweed coat of hers was a cheap affair; it didn't keep the cold out. He could put it so that she wouldn't mind, perhaps . . .

They must have another evening out soon. It was a pleasure to take a girl like that to a smart restaurant. He could see several young fellows were envying him. She was uncommonly pretty. And she liked him. To her, as she had told him, he didn't seem a bit old.

He looked up and caught his wife's eye. He felt suddenly guilty, which annoyed him. What a narrow-minded, suspicious woman Maria was! She grudged him any little bit of happiness.

He switched off the radio and went to bed.

Mrs Packington received two unexpected letters the following morning. One was a printed form confirming an appointment at a noted beauty specialist's. The second was an appointment with a dressmaker. The third was from Mr Parker Pyne, requesting the pleasure of her company at lunch at the Ritz that day.

Mr Packington mentioned that he might not be home to dinner that evening as he had to see a man on business. Mrs Packington merely nodded absently, and Mr Packington left the house congratulating himself on having escaped the storm.

The beauty specialist was impressive. Such neglect! Madame, but *why*? This should have been taken in hand years ago. However, it was not too late.

Things were done to her face; it was pressed and kneaded and steamed. It had mud applied to it. It had creams applied to it. It was dusted with powder. There were various finishing touches.

At last she was given a mirror. 'I believe I *do* look younger,' she thought to herself.

The dressmaking seance was equally exciting. She emerged feeling smart, modish, up-to-date.

At half-past one, Mrs Packington kept her appointment at the Ritz. Mr Parker Pyne, faultlessly dressed and carrying with him his atmosphere of soothing reassurance, was waiting for her.

'Charming,' he said, an experienced eye sweeping her from head to foot. 'I have ventured to order you a White Lady.'

Mrs Packington, who had not contracted the cocktail habit, made no demur. As she sipped the exciting fluid gingerly, she listened to her benevolent instructor.

'Your husband, Mrs Packington,' said Mr Parker Pyne, 'must be made to Sit Up. You understand – to Sit Up. To assist in that, I am going to introduce to you a young friend of mine. You will lunch with him today.'

At that moment a young man came along, looking from side to side. He espied Mr Parker Pyne and came gracefully towards them.

'Mr Claude Luttrell, Mrs Packington.'

Mr Claude Luttrell was perhaps just short of thirty. He was graceful, debonair, perfectly dressed, extremely handsome.

'Delighted to meet you,' he murmured.

Three minutes later Mrs Packington was facing her new mentor at a small table for two.

She was shy at first, but Mr Luttrell soon put her at her ease. He knew Paris well and had spent a good deal of time on the Riviera. He asked Mrs Packington if she were fond of dancing. Mrs Packington said she was, but that she seldom got any dancing nowadays as Mr Packington didn't care to go out in the evenings.

'But he couldn't be so unkind as to keep *you* at home,' said Claude Luttrell, smiling and displaying a dazzling row of teeth. 'Women will not tolerate male jealousy in these days.'

Mrs Packington nearly said that jealousy didn't enter into the question. But the words remained unspoken. After all, it was an agreeable idea.

Claude Luttrell spoke airily of night clubs. It was settled that on the following evening Mrs Packington and Mr Luttrell should patronize the popular Lesser Archangel.

Mrs Packington was a little nervous about announcing this fact to her husband. George, she felt, would think it extraordinary and possibly ridiculous. But she was saved all trouble on this score. She had been too nervous to make her announcement at breakfast, and at two o'clock a telephone message came to the effect that Mr Packington would be dining in town.

The evening was a great success. Mrs Packington had been a good dancer as a girl and under Claude Luttrell's skilled guidance she soon picked up modern steps. He congratulated her on her gown and also on the arrangement of her hair. (An appointment had been made for her that morning with a fashionable hairdresser.) On bidding her farewell, he kissed her hand in a most thrilling manner. Mrs Packington had not enjoyed an evening so much for years.

A bewildering ten days ensued. Mrs Packington lunched, teaed, tangoed, dined, danced and supped. She heard all about Claude Luttrell's sad childhood. She heard the sad circumstances in which his father lost all his money. She heard of his tragic romance and his embittered feelings towards women generally.

On the eleventh day they were dancing at the Red Admiral. Mrs Packington saw her spouse before he saw her. George was with the young lady from his office. Both couples were dancing.

'Hallo, George,' said Mrs Packington lightly, as their orbits brought them together.

It was with considerable amusement that she saw her husband's face grow first red, then purple with astonishment. With the astonishment was blended an expression of guilt detected.

Mrs Packington felt amusedly mistress of the situation. Poor old George! Seated once more at her table, she watched them. How stout he was, how bald, how terribly he bounced on his feet! He danced in the style of twenty years ago. Poor George, how terribly he wanted to be young! And that poor girl he was dancing with had to pretend to like it. She looked bored enough now, her face over his shoulder where he couldn't see it.

How much more enviable, thought Mrs Packington contentedly, was her own situation. She glanced at the perfect Claude, now tactfully silent. How well he understood her. He never jarred – as husbands so inevitably did jar after a lapse of years.

She looked at him again. Their eyes met. He smiled; his beautiful dark eyes, so melancholy, so romantic, looked tenderly into hers.

'Shall we dance again?' he murmured.

They danced again. It was heaven!

She was conscious of George's apoplectic gaze following them. It had been the idea, she remembered, to make George jealous. What a long time ago that was! She really didn't want George to be jealous now. It might upset him. Why should he be upset, poor thing? Every one was so happy. . . .

Mr Packington had been home an hour when Mrs Packington got in. He looked bewildered and unsure of himself.

'Humph,' he remarked. 'So you're back.'

Mrs Packington cast off an evening wrap which had cost her forty guineas that very morning. 'Yes,' she said, smiling. 'I'm back.'

George coughed. 'Er – rather odd meeting you.'

'Wasn't it?' said Mrs Packington.

'I – well, I thought it would be a kindness to take that girl somewhere. She's been having a lot of trouble at home. I thought – well, kindness, you know.'

Mrs Packington nodded. Poor old George – bouncing on his feet and getting so hot and being so pleased with himself.

'Who's that chap you were with? I don't know him, do I?'

'Luttrell, his name is. Claude Luttrell.'

'How did you come across him?'

'Oh, some one introduced me,' said Mrs Packington vaguely.

'Rather a queer thing for you to go out dancing – at your time of life. Mustn't make a fool of yourself, my dear.'

Mrs Packington smiled. She was feeling much too kindly to the universe in general to make the obvious reply. 'A change is always nice,' she said amiably.

'You've got to be careful, you know. A lot of these lounge-lizard fellows going about. Middle-aged women sometimes make awful fools of themselves. I'm just warning you, my dear. I don't like to see you doing anything unsuitable.'

'I find the exercise beneficial,' said Mrs Packington.

'Um – yes.'

'I expect you do, too,' said Mrs Packington kindly. 'The great thing is to be happy, isn't it? I remember your saying so one morning at breakfast, about ten days ago.'

Her husband looked at her sharply, but her expression was devoid of sarcasm. She yawned.

'I must go to bed. By the way, George, I've been dreadfully extravagant lately. Some terrible bills will be coming in. You don't mind, do you?'

'Bills?' said Mr Packington.

'Yes. For clothes. And massage. And hair treatment. Wickedly extravagant I've been – but I know you won't mind.'

She passed up the stairs. Mr Packington remained with his mouth open. Maria had been amazingly nice about this evening's business; she hadn't seemed to care at all. But it was a pity she had suddenly taken to spending Money. Maria – the model of economy!

Women! George Packington shook his head. The scrapes that girl's brother had been getting into lately. Well, he'd been glad to help. All the same – and dash it all, things weren't going too well in the city.

Sighing, Mr Packington in his turn slowly climbed the stairs.

Sometimes words that fail to make their effect at the time are remembered later. Not till the following morning did certain words uttered by Mr Packington really penetrate his wife's consciousness.

Lounge lizards; middle-aged women; awful fools of themselves.

Mrs Packington was courageous at heart. She sat down and faced facts. A gigolo. She had read all about gigolos in the papers. Had read, too, of the follies of middle-aged women.

Was Claude a gigolo? She supposed he was. But then, gigolos were paid for and Claude always paid for her. Yes, but it was Mr Parker Pyne who paid, not Claude – or, rather, it was really her own two hundred guineas.

Was she a middle-aged fool? Did Claude Luttrell laugh at her behind her back? Her face flushed at the thought.

Well, what of it? Claude was a gigolo. She was a middle-aged fool. She supposed she should have given him something. A gold cigarette case. That sort of thing.

A queer impulse drove her out there and then to Asprey's. The cigarette case was chosen and paid for. She was to meet Claude at Claridge's for lunch.

As they were sipping coffee she produced it from her bag. 'A little present,' she murmured.

He looked up, frowned. 'For me?'

'Yes. I – I hope you like it.'

His hand closed over it and he slid it violently across the table. 'Why do you give me that? I won't take it. Take it back. Take it back, I say.' He was angry. His dark eyes flashed.

She murmured, 'I'm sorry,' and put it away in her bag again.

There was constraint between them that day.

The following morning he rang her up. 'I must see you. Can I come to your house this afternoon?'

She told him to come at three o'clock.

He arrived very white, very tense. They greeted each other. The constraint was more evident.

Suddenly he sprang up and stood facing her. 'What do you think I am? That is what I've come to ask you. We've been friends, haven't we? Yes, friends. But all the same, you think I'm – well, a gigolo. A creature who lives on women. A lounge lizard. You do, don't you?'

'No, no.'

He swept aside her protest. His face had gone very white. 'You *do* think that! Well, it's true. That's what I've come to say. It's true! I had my orders to take you about, to amuse you, to make love to you, to make you forget your husband. That was my job. A despicable one, eh?'

'Why are you telling me this?' she asked.

'Because I'm through with it. I can't carry on with it. Not with *you*. You're different. You're the kind of woman I could believe in, trust, adore. You think I'm just saying this; that it's part of the game.' He came closer to her. 'I'm going to prove to you it isn't. I'm going away – because of you. I'm going to make myself into a man instead of the loathsome creature I am because of you.'

He took her suddenly in his arms. His lips closed on hers. Then he released her and stood away.

'Goodbye. I've been a rotter – always. But I swear it will be different now. Do you remember once saying you liked to read the advertisements in the Agony column? On this day ever year you'll find there a message from me saying that I remember and am making good. You'll know, then, all you've meant to me. One thing more. I've taken nothing from you. I want you to take something from me.' He drew a plain gold seal ring from his finger. 'This was my mother's. I'd like you to have it. Now goodbye.'

He left her standing there amazed, the gold ring in her hand.

George Packington came home early. He found his wife gazing into the fire with a faraway look. She spoke kindly but absently to him.

'Look here, Maria,' he jerked out suddenly. 'About that girl?'

'Yes, dear?'

'I – I never meant to upset you, you know. About her. Nothing in it.'

'I know. I was foolish. See as much as you like of her if it makes you happy.'

These words, surely, should have cheered George Packington. Strangely enough, they annoyed him. How could you enjoy taking a girl about when your wife fairly urged you on? Dash it all, it wasn't decent! All that feeling of being a gay dog, of being a strong man playing with fire, fizzled out and died an ignominious death. George Packington felt suddenly tired and a great deal poorer in pocket. The girl was a shrewd little piece.

'We might go away together somewhere for a bit if you like, Maria?' he suggested timidly.

'Oh, never mind about me. I'm quite happy.'

'But I'd like to take you away. We might go to the Riviera.'

Mrs Packington smiled at him from a distance.

Poor old George. She was fond of him. He was such a pathetic old dear. There was no secret splendour in his life as there was in hers. She smiled more tenderly still.

'That would be lovely, my dear,' she said.

Mr Parker Pyne was speaking to Miss Lemon. 'Entertainment account?'

'One hundred and two pounds, fourteen and sixpence,' said Miss Lemon.

The door was pushed open and Claude Luttrell entered. He looked moody.

'Morning, Claude,' said Mr Parker Pyne. 'Everything go off satisfactorily?'

'I suppose so.'

'The ring? What name did you put in it, by the way?'

'Matilda,' said Claude gloomily. '1899.'

'Excellent. What wording for the advertisement?'

'"Making good. Still remember. Claude."'

'Make a note of that please, Miss Lemon. The Agony column. November third for – let me see, expenses a hundred and two pounds, fourteen and six. Yes, for ten years, I think. That leaves us a profit of ninety-two pounds, two and fourpence. Adequate. Quite adequate.'

Miss Lemon departed.

'Look here,' Claude burst out. 'I don't like this. It's a rotten game.'

'My dear boy.'

'A rotten game. That was a decent woman – a good sort. Telling her all those lies, filling her up with this sob-stuff, dash it all, it makes me sick!'

Mr Parker Pyne adjusted his glasses and looked at Claude with a kind of scientific interest. 'Dear me!' he said dryly. 'I do not seem to remember that your conscience ever troubled you during your somewhat – ahem! – notorious career. Your affairs on the Riviera were particularly brazen, and your exploitation of Mrs Hattie West, the Californian Cucumber King's wife, was especially notable for the callous mercenary instinct you displayed.'

'Well, I'm beginning to feel different,' grumbled Claude. 'It isn't – nice, this game.'

Mr Parker Pyne spoke in the voice of a head master admonishing a favourite pupil. 'You have, my dear Claude, performed a meritorious action. You have given an unhappy woman what every woman needs – a romance. A woman tears a passion to pieces and gets no good from it, but a romance can be laid up in lavender and looked at all through the long years to come. I know human nature, my dear boy, and I tell you that a woman can feed on such an incident for years.' He coughed. 'We have discharged our commission to Mrs Packington very satisfactorily.'

'Well,' muttered Claude, 'I don't like it.' He left the room.

Mr Parker Pyne took a new file from a drawer. He wrote: 'Interesting vestiges of a conscience noticeable in hardened Lounge Lizard. Note: Study developments.'

The Mystery of the Blue Jar

Jack Hartington surveyed his topped drive ruefully. Standing by the ball, he looked back to the tee, measuring the distance. His face was eloquent of the disgusted contempt which he felt. With a sigh he drew out his iron, executed two vicious swings with it, annihilating in turn a dandelion and a tuft of grass, and then addressed himself firmly to the ball.

It is hard when you are twenty-four years of age, and your one ambition in life is to reduce your handicap at golf, to be forced to give time and attention to the problem of earning your living. Five and a half days out of the seven saw Jack imprisoned in a kind of mahogany tomb in the city. Saturday afternoon and Sunday were religiously devoted to the real business of life, and in an excess of zeal he had taken rooms at the small hotel near Stourton Heath links, and rose daily at the hour of six a.m. to get in an hour's practice before catching the 8.46 to town.

The only disadvantage to the plan was that he seemed constitutionally unable to hit anything at that hour in the morning. A foozled iron succeeded a muffed drive. His mashie shots ran merrily along the ground, and four putts seemed to be the minimum on any green.

Jack sighed, grasped his iron firmly and repeated to himself the magic words, 'Left arm right through, and don't look up.'

He swung back – and then stopped, petrified, as a shrill cry rent the silence of the summer's morning.

'Murder,' it called. 'Help! Murder!'

It was a woman's voice, and it died away at the end into a sort of gurgling sigh.

Jack flung down his club and ran in the direction of the sound. It had come from somewhere quite near at hand. This particular part of the course was quite wild country, and there were few houses about. In fact, there was only one near at hand, a small picturesque cottage, which Jack had often noticed for its air of old world daintiness. It was towards this cottage that he ran. It was hidden from him by a heather-covered slope, but he rounded this and in less than a minute was standing with his hand on the small latched gate.

There was a girl standing in the garden, and for a moment Jack jumped to the natural conclusion that it was she who had uttered the cry for help. But he quickly changed his mind.

She had a little basket in her hand, half full of weeds, and had evidently just straightened herself up from weeding a wide border of pansies. Her eyes, Jack noticed, were just like pansies themselves, velvety and soft and dark, and more violet than blue. She was like a pansy altogether, in her straight purple linen gown.

The girl was looking at Jack with an expression midway between annoyance and surprise.

'I beg your pardon,' said the young man. 'But did you cry out just now?'

'I? No, indeed.'

Her surprise was so genuine that Jack felt confused. Her voice was very soft and pretty with a slight foreign inflection.

'But you must have heard it,' he exclaimed. 'It came from somewhere just near here.'

She stared at him.

'I heard nothing at all.'

Jack in his turn stared at her. It was perfectly incredible that she should not have heard that agonized appeal for help. And yet her calmness was so evident that he could not believe she was lying to him.

'It came from somewhere close at hand,' he insisted.

She was looking at him suspiciously now.

'What did it say?' she asked.

'Murder – help! Murder!'

'Murder – help, murder,' repeated the girl. 'Somebody has played a trick on you, Monsieur. Who could be murdered here?'

Jack looked about him with a confused idea of discovering a dead body upon a garden path. Yet he was still perfectly sure that the cry he had heard was real and not a product of his imagination. He looked up at the cottage windows. Everything seemed perfectly still and peaceful.

'Do you want to search our house?' asked the girl dryly.

She was so clearly sceptical that Jack's confusion grew deeper than ever. He turned away.

'I'm sorry,' he said. 'It must have come from higher up in the woods.'

He raised his cap and retreated. Glancing back over his shoulder, he saw that the girl had calmly resumed her weeding.

For some time he hunted through the woods, but could find no sign of anything unusual having occurred. Yet he was as positive as ever that he had really heard the cry. In the end, he gave up the search and hurried home to bolt his breakfast and catch the 8.46 by the usual narrow margin of a second or so. His conscience pricked him a little as he sat in the train. Ought he not to have immediately reported what he had heard to the police? That he had not done so was solely owing to the pansy girl's incredulity. She had clearly suspected him of romancing – possibly the police might do the same. *Was* he absolutely certain that he had heard the cry?

By now he was not nearly so positive as he had been – the natural result of trying to recapture a lost sensation. Was it some bird's cry in the distance that he had twisted into the semblance of a woman's voice?

But he rejected the suggestion angrily. It was a woman's voice, and he had heard it. He remembered looking at his watch just before the cry had come. As nearly as possible it must have been five and twenty minutes past seven when he had heard the call. That might be a fact useful to the police if – if anything should be discovered.

Going home that evening, he scanned the evening papers anxiously to see if there were any mention of a crime having been committed. But there was nothing, and he hardly knew whether to be relieved or disappointed.

The following morning was wet – so wet that even the most ardent golfer might have his enthusiasm damped. Jack rose at the last possible moment, gulped his breakfast, ran for the train and again eagerly scanned the papers. Still no mention of any gruesome discovery having been made. The evening papers told the same tale.

'Queer,' said Jack to himself, 'but there it is. Probably some blinking little boys having a game together up in the woods.'

He was out early the following morning. As he passed the cottage, he noted out the tail of his eye that the girl was out in the garden again weeding. Evidently a habit of hers. He did a particularly good approach shot, and hoped that she had noticed it. As he teed up on the next tee, he glanced at his watch.

'Just five and twenty past seven,' he murmured. 'I wonder——'

The words were frozen on his lips. From behind him came the same cry which had so startled him before. A woman's voice, in dire distress.

'Murder – help! Murder!'

Jack raced back. The pansy girl was standing by the gate.

She looked startled, and Jack ran up to her triumphantly, crying out:

'You heard it this time, anyway.'

Her eyes were wide with some emotion he could not fathom but he noticed that she shrank back from him as he approached, and even glanced back at the house, as though she meditated running to it for shelter.

She shook her head, staring at him.

'I heard nothing at all,' she said wonderingly.

It was as though she had struck him a blow between the eyes. Her sincerity was so evident that he could not disbelieve her. Yet he couldn't have imagined it – he couldn't – he couldn't——

He heard her voice speaking gently – almost with sympathy.

'You have had the shellshock, yes?'

In a flash he understood her look of fear, her glance back at the house. She thought that he suffered from delusions. . . .

And then, like a douche of cold water, came the horrible thought, was she right? *Did* he suffer from delusions? Obsessed by the horror of the thought, he turned and stumbled away without vouchsafing a word. The girl watched him go, sighed, shook her head, and bent down to her weeding again.

Jack endeavoured to reason matters out with himself. 'If I hear the damned thing again at twenty-five minutes past seven,' he said to himself, 'it is clear that I've got hold of a hallucination of some sort. But I won't hear it.'

He was nervous all that day, and went to bed early determined to put the matter to the proof the following morning.

As was perhaps natural in such a case, he remained awake half the night, and finally overslept himself. It was twenty past seven by the time he was clear of the hotel and running towards the links. He realized that he would not be able to get to the fatal spot by twenty-five past, but surely, if the voice was a hallucination pure and simple, he would hear it anywhere. He ran on, his eyes fixed on the hands of his watch.

Twenty-five past. From far off came the echo of a woman's voice calling. The words could not be distinguished, but he was convinced that it was the same cry he had heard before, and that it came from the same spot, somewhere in the neighbourhood of the cottage.

Strangely enough, that fact reassured him. It might, after all, be a hoax. Unlikely as it seemed, the girl herself might be playing a trick on him. He set his shoulders resolutely, and took out a club from his golf bag. He would play the few holes up to the cottage.

The girl was in the garden as usual. She looked up this morning, and when he raised his cap to her, said good morning rather shyly. . . . She looked, he thought, lovelier than ever.

'Nice day, isn't it?' Jack called out cheerily, cursing the unavoidable banality of the observation.

'Yes, indeed, it is lovely.'

'Good for the garden, I expect?'

The girl smiled a little, disclosing a fascinating dimple.

'Alas, no! For my flowers the rain is needed. See, they are all dried up.'

Jack accepted the invitation of her gesture, and came up to the low hedge dividing the garden from the course, looking over it into the garden.

'They seem all right,' he remarked awkwardly, conscious as he spoke of the girl's slightly pitying glance running over him.

'The sun is good, is it not?' she said. 'For the flowers one can always water them. But the sun gives strength and repairs the health. Monsieur is much better today, I can see.'

Her encouraging tone annoyed Jack intensely.

'Curse it all,' he said to himself. 'I believe she's trying to cure me by suggestion.'

'I'm perfectly well,' he said.

'That is good then,' returned the girl quickly and soothingly.

Jack had the irritating feeling that she didn't believe him.

He played a few more holes and hurried back to breakfast. As he ate it, he was conscious, not for the first time, of the close scrutiny of a man who sat at the table next to him. He was a man of middle-age, with a powerful forceful face. He had a small dark beard and very piercing grey eyes, and an ease and assurance of manner which placed him among the higher ranks of the professional classes. His name, Jack knew, was Lavington, and he had heard vague rumours as to his being a well-known medical specialist, but as Jack was not a frequenter of Harley Street, the name had conveyed little or nothing to him.

But this morning he was very conscious of the quiet observation under which he was being kept, and it frightened him a little. Was his secret written plainly in his face for all to see? Did this man, by reason of his professional calling, know that there was something amiss in the hidden grey matter.

Jack shivered at the thought. Was it true? Was he really going mad? Was the whole thing a hallucination, or was it a gigantic hoax?

And suddenly a very simple way of testing the solution occurred to him. He had hitherto been alone on his round. Supposing someone else was with him? Then one out of three things might happen. The voice might be silent. They might both hear it. Or – he only might hear it.

That evening he proceeded to carry his plan into effect. Lavington was the man he wanted with him. They fell into conversation easily enough – the older man might have been waiting for such an opening. It was clear that for some reason or other Jack interested him. The latter was able to come quite easily and naturally to the suggestion that they might play a few holes together before breakfast. The arrangement was made for the following morning.

They started out a little before seven. It was a perfect day, still and cloudless, but not too warm. The doctor was playing well, Jack wretchedly. His whole mind was intent on the forthcoming crisis. He kept glancing surreptitiously at his watch. They reached the seventh tee, between which and the hole the cottage was situated, about twenty past seven.

The girl, as usual, was in the garden as they passed. She did not look up.

The two balls lay on the green, Jack's near the hole, the doctor's some little distance away.

'I've got this for it,' said Lavington. 'I must go for it, I suppose.'

He bent down, judging the line he should take. Jack stood rigid, his eyes glued on his watch. It was exactly twenty-five minutes past seven.

The ball ran swiftly along the grass, stopped on the edge of the hole, hesitated and dropped in.

'Good putt,' said Jack. His voice sounded hoarse and unlike himself. . . . He shoved his wrist watch farther up his arm with a sigh of overwhelming relief. Nothing had happened. The spell was broken.

'If you don't mind waiting a minute,' he said, 'I think I'll have a pipe.'

They paused a while on the eighth tee. Jack filled and lit the pipe with fingers that trembled a little in spite of himself. An enormous weight seemed to have lifted from his mind.

'Lord, what a good day it is,' he remarked, staring at the prospect ahead of him with great contentment. 'Go on, Lavington, your swipe.'

And then it came. Just at the very instant the doctor was hitting. A woman's voice, high and agonized.

'Murder – Help! Murder!'

The pipe fell from Jack's nerveless hand, as he spun round in the direction of the sound, and then, remembering, gazed breathlessly at his companion.

Lavington was looking down the course, shading his eyes.

'A bit short – just cleared the bunker, though, I think.'

He had heard nothing.

The world seemed to spin round with Jack. He took a step or two, lurching heavily. When he recovered himself, he was lying on the short turf, and Lavington was bending over him.

'There, take it easy now, take it easy.'

'What did I do?'

'You fainted, young man – or gave a very good try at it.'

'My God!' said Jack, and groaned.

'What's the trouble? Something on your mind?'

'I'll tell you in one minute, but I'd like to ask you something first.'

The doctor lit his own pipe and settled himself on the bank.

'Ask anything you like,' he said comfortably.

'You've been watching me for the last day or two. Why?'

Lavington's eyes twinkled a little.

'That's rather an awkward question. A cat can look at a king, you know.'

'Don't put me off. I'm earnest. Why was it? I've a vital reason for asking.'

Lavington's face grew serious.

'I'll answer you quite honestly. I recognized in you all the signs of a man labouring under a sense of acute strain, and it intrigued me what that strain could be.'

'I can tell you easily enough,' said Jack bitterly. 'I'm going mad.'

He stopped dramatically, but his statement not seeming to arouse the interest and consternation he expected, he repeated it.

'I tell you I'm going mad.'

'Very curious,' murmured Lavington. 'Very curious indeed.'

Jack felt indignant.

'I suppose that's all it does seem to you. Doctors are so damned callous.'

'Come, come my young friend, you're talking at random. To begin with, although I have taken my degree, I do not practise medicine. Strictly speaking, I am not a doctor – not a doctor of the body, that is.'

Jack looked at him keenly.

'Or the mind?'

'Yes, in a sense, but more truly I call myself a doctor of the soul.'

'Oh!'

'I perceive the disparagement in your tone, and yet we must use some word to denote the active principle which can be separated and exist independently of its fleshly home, the body. You've got to come to terms with the soul, you know, young man, it isn't just a religious term invented by clergymen. But we'll call it the mind, or the subconscious self, or any term that suits you better. You took offence at my tone just now, but I can assure you that it really did strike me as very curious that such a well-balanced and perfectly normal young man as yourself should suffer from the delusion that he was going out of his mind.'

'I'm out of my mind all right. Absolutely balmy.'

'You will forgive me for saying so, but I don't believe it.'

'I suffer from delusions.'

'After dinner?'

'No, in the morning.'

'Can't be done,' said the doctor, relighting his pipe which had gone out.

'I tell you I hear things that no one else hears.'

'One man in a thousand can see the moons of Jupiter. Because the other nine hundred and ninety nine can't see them there's no reason to doubt that the moons of Jupiter exist, and certainly no reason for calling the thousandth man a lunatic.'

'The moons of Jupiter are a proved scientific fact.'

'It's quite possible that the delusions today may be the proved scientific facts tomorrow.'

In spite of himself, Lavington's matter-of-fact manner was having its effect upon Jack. He felt immeasurably soothed and cheered. The doctor looked at him attentively for a minute or two and then nodded.

'That's better,' he said. 'The trouble with you young fellows is that you're so cocksure nothing can exist outside your own philosophy that you get the wind up when something occurs to jolt you out of that opinion. Let's hear your grounds for believing that you're going mad, and we'll decide whether or not to lock you up afterwards.'

As faithfully as he could, Jack narrated the whole series of occurrences.

'But what I can't understand,' he ended, 'is why this morning it should come at half past seven – five minutes late.

Lavington thought for a minute or two. Then——

'What's the time now by your watch?' he asked.

'Quarter to eight,' replied Jack, consulting it.

'That's simple enough, then. Mine says twenty to eight. Your watch is five minutes fast. That's a very interesting and important point – to me. In fact, it's invaluable.'

'In what way?'

Jack was beginning to get interested.

'Well, the obvious explanation is that on the first morning you *did* hear some such cry – may have been a joke, may not. On the following mornings, you suggestioned yourself to hear it at exactly the same time.'

'I'm sure I didn't.'

'Not consciously, of course, but the subconscious plays us some funny tricks, you know. But anyway, that explanation won't wash. If it was a cause of suggestion, you would have heard the cry at twenty-five minutes past seven by your watch, and you could never have heard it when the time, as you thought, was past.'

'Well, then?'

'Well – it's obvious, isn't it? This cry for help occupies a perfectly definite place and time in space. The place is the vicinity of that cottage and the time is twenty-five minutes past seven.'

'Yes, but why should *I* be the one to hear it? I don't believe in ghosts and all that spook stuff – spirits rapping and all the rest of it. Why should I hear the damned thing?'

'Ah! that we can't tell at present. It's a curious thing that many of the best mediums are made out of confirmed sceptics. It isn't the people who are interested in occult phenomena who get the manifestations. Some people see and hear things that other people don't – we don't know why, and nine times out of ten they don't want to see or hear them, and are convinced that they are suffering from delusions – just as you were. It's like electricity. Some substances are good conductors, others are non-conductors, and for a long time we didn't know why, and had to be content just to accept the fact. Nowadays we do know why. Some day, no doubt, we shall know why you hear this thing and I and the girl don't. Everything's governed by the natural law, you know – there's no such thing really as the supernatural. Finding out the laws that govern so called psychic phenomena is going to be a tough job – but every little helps.'

'But what am I going to *do*?' asked Jack.

Lavington chuckled.

'Practical, I see. Well, my young friend, you are going to have a good breakfast and get off to the city without worrying your head further about things you don't understand. I, on the other hand, am going to poke about, and see what I can find out about that cottage back there. That's where the mystery centres, I dare swear.'

Jack rose to his feet.

'Right, sir, I'm on, but, I say——'

'Yes?'

Jack flushed awkwardly.

'I'm sure the girl's all right,' he muttered.

Lavington looked amused.

'You didn't tell me she was a pretty girl! Well, cheer up, I think the mystery started before her time.'

Jack arrived home that evening in a perfect fever of curiosity. He was by now pinning his faith blindly to Lavington. The doctor had accepted the matter so naturally, had been so matter-of-fact and unperturbed by it, that Jack was impressed.

He found his new friend waiting for him in the hall when he came down for dinner, and the doctor suggested that they should dine together at the same table.

'Any news, sir?' asked Jack anxiously.

'I've collected the life history of Heather Cottage all right. It was tenanted first by an old gardener and his wife. The old man died, and the old woman went to her daughter. Then a builder got hold of it, and modernized it with great success, selling it to a city gentleman who used it for weekends. About a year ago, he sold it to some people called Turner – Mr and Mrs Turner. They seem to have been rather a curious couple from all I can make out. He was an Englishman, his wife was popularly supposed to be partly Russian, and was a very handsome exotic-looking woman. They lived very quietly, seeing no one, and hardly ever going outside the cottage garden. The local rumour goes that they were afraid of something – but I don't think we ought to rely on that.

'And then suddenly one day they departed, cleared out one morning early, and never came back. The agents here got a letter from Mr Turner, written from London, instructing him to sell up the place as quickly as possible. The furniture was sold off, and the house itself was sold to a Mr Mauleverer. He only actually lived in it a fortnight – then he advertised it to be let furnished. The people who have it now are a consumptive French professor and his daughter. They have been there just ten days.'

Jack digested this in silence.

'I don't see that that gets us any forrader,' he said at last. 'Do you?'

'I rather want to know more about the Turners,' said

Lavington quietly. 'They left very early in the morning, you remember. As far as I can make out, nobody actually saw them go. Mr Turner has been seen since – but I can't find anybody who has seen Mrs Turner.'

Jack paled.

'It can't be – you don't mean——'

'Don't excite yourself, young man. The influence of anyone at the point of death – and especially of violent death – upon their surroundings is very strong. Those surroundings might conceivably absorb that influence, transmitting it in turn to a suitably tuned receiver – in this case yourself.'

'But why me?' murmured Jack rebelliously. 'Why not someone who could do some good?'

'You are regarding the force as intelligent and purposeful, instead of blind and mechanical. I do not believe myself in earthbound spirits, haunting a spot for one particular purpose. But the thing I have seen, again and again, until I can hardly believe it to be pure coincidence, is a kind of blind groping towards justice – a subterranean moving of blind forces, always working obscurely towards that end. . . .'

He shook himself – as though casting off some obsession that preoccupied him, and turned to Jack with a ready smile.

'Let us banish the subject – for tonight at all events,' he suggested.

Jack agreed readily enough, but did not find it so easy to banish the subject from his own mind.

During the weekend, he made vigorous inquiries of his own, but succeeded in eliciting little more than the doctor had done. He had definitely given up playing golf before breakfast.

The next link in the chain came from an unexpected quarter. On getting back one day, Jack was informed that a young lady was waiting to see him. To his intense surprise it proved to be the girl of the garden – the pansy girl, as he always called her in his own mind. She was very nervous and confused.

'You will forgive me, Monsieur, for coming to seek you like this? But there is something I want to tell you – I——'

She looked round uncertainly.

'Come in here,' said Jack promptly, leading the way into the now deserted 'Ladies' Drawing-room' of the hotel, a dreary apartment, with a good deal of red plush about it. 'Now, sit down, Miss, Miss——'

'Marchaud, Monsieur. Felise Marchaud.'

'Sit down, Mademoiselle Marchaud, and tell me all about it.'

Felice sat down obediently. She was dressed in dark green today, and the beauty and charm of the proud little face was more evident than ever. Jack's heart beat faster as he sat down beside her.

'It is like this,' explained Felise. 'We have been here but a short time, and from the beginning we hear the house – our so sweet little house – is haunted. No servant will stay in it. That does not matter so much – me, I can do the *ménage* and cook easily enough.'

'Angel,' thought the infatuated young man. 'She's wonderful.'

But he maintained an outward semblance of businesslike attention.

'This talk of ghosts, I think it is all folly – that is until four days ago. Monsieur, four nights running, I have had the same dream. A lady stands there – she is beautiful, tall and very fair. In her hands she holds a blue china jar. She is distressed – very distressed, and continually she holds out the jar to me, as though imploring me to do something with it – but alas! she cannot speak, and I – I do not know what she asks. That was the dream for the first two nights – but the night before last, there was more of it. She and the blue jar faded away, and suddenly I heard her voice crying out – I know it is her voice, you comprehend – and, oh! Monsieur, the words she says are those you spoke to me that morning. "Murder – Help! Murder!" I awoke in terror. I say to myself

– it is a nightmare, the words you heard are an accident. But last night the dream came again. Monsieur, what is it? You too have heard. What shall we do?'

Felise's face was terrified. Her small hands clasped themselves together, and she gazed appealingly at Jack. The latter affected an unconcern he did not feel.

'That's all right, Mademoiselle Marchaud. You mustn't worry. I tell you what I'd like you to do, if you don't mind, repeat the whole story to a friend of mine who is staying here, a Dr Lavington.

Felise signified her willingness to adopt this course, and Jack went off in search of Lavington. He returned with him a few minutes later.

Lavington gave the girl a keen scrutiny as he acknowledged Jack's hurried introductions. With a few reassuring words, he soon put the girl at her ease, and he, in his turn, listened attentively to her story.

'Very curious,' he said, when she had finished. 'You have told your father of this?'

Felise shook her head.

'I have not liked to worry him. He is very ill still' – her eyes filled with tears – 'I keep from him anything that might excite or agitate him.'

'I understand,' said Lavington kindly. 'And I am glad you came to us, Mademoiselle Marchaud. Hartington here, as you know, had an experience something similar to yours. I think I may say that we are well on the track now. There is nothing else that you can think of?'

Felise gave a quick movement.

'Of course! How stupid I am. It is the point of the whole story. Look, Monsieur, at what I found at the back of one of the cupboards where it had slipped behind the shelf.'

She held out to them a dirty piece of drawing-paper on which was executed roughly in water colours a sketch of a woman. It was a mere daub, but the likeness was probably good enough. It represented a tall fair woman, with something subtly un-English in her face. She was standing by a table on which was standing a blue china jar.

'I only found it this morning,' explained Felise. 'Monsieur le docteur, that is the face of the woman I saw in my dream, and that is the identical blue jar.'

'Extraordinary,' commented Lavington. 'The key to the mystery is evidently the blue jar. It looks like a Chinese jar to me, probably an old one. It seems to have a curious raised pattern over it.'

'It is Chinese,' declared Jack. 'I have seen an exactly similar one in my uncle's collection – he is a great collector of Chinese porcelain, you know, and I remember noticing a jar just like this a short time ago.'

'The Chinese jar,' mused Lavington. He remained a minute or two lost in thought, then raised his head suddenly, a curious light shining in his eyes. 'Hartington, how long has your uncle had that jar?'

'How long? I really don't know.'

'Think. Did he buy it lately?'

'I don't know – yes, I believe he did, now I come to think of it. I'm not very interested in porcelain myself, but I remember his showing me his "recent acquisitions," and this was one of them.'

'Less than two months ago? The Turners left Heather Cottage just two months ago.'

'Yes, I believe it was.'

'Your uncle attends country sales sometimes?'

'He's always tooling round to sales.'

'Then there is no inherent improbability in our assuming that he bought this particular piece of porcelain at the sale of the Turners' things. A curious coincidence – or perhaps what I call the groping of blind justice. Hartington, you must find out from your uncle at once where he bought this jar.'

Jack's face fell.

'I'm afraid that's impossible. Uncle George is away on the Continent. I don't even know where to write to him.'

'How long will he be away?'

'Three weeks to a month at least.'

There was silence. Felise sat looking anxiously from one man to the other.

'Is there nothing that we can do?' she asked timidly.

'Yes, there is one thing,' said Lavington, in a tone of suppressed excitement. 'It is unusual, perhaps, but I believe that it will succeed. Hartington, you must get hold of that jar. Bring it down here, and, if Mademoiselle permits, we will spend a night in Heather Cottage, taking the blue jar with us.'

Jack felt his skin creep uncomfortably.

'What do you think will happen?' he asked uneasily.

'I have not the slightest idea – but I honestly believe that the mystery will be solved and the ghost laid. Quite possibly there may be a false bottom to the jar and something is concealed inside it. If no phenomena occur, we must use our own ingenuity.

Felise clasped her hands.

'It is a wonderful idea,' she exclaimed.

Her eyes were alight with enthusiasm. Jack did not feel nearly so enthusiastic – in fact, he was inwardly funking it badly, but nothing would have induced him to admit the fact before Felise. The doctor acted as though his suggestion were the most natural one in the world.

'When can you get the jar?' asked Felise, turning to Jack.

'Tomorrow,' said the latter, unwillingly.

He had to go through with it now, but the memory of the frenzied cry for help that had haunted him each morning was something to be ruthlessly thrust down and not thought about more than could be helped.

He went to his uncle's house the following evening, and took away the jar in question. He was more than ever convinced when he saw it again that it was the identical one pictured in the water colour sketch, but carefully as he looked it over he could see no sign that it contained a secret receptacle of any kind.

It was eleven o'clock when he and Lavington arrived at Heather Cottage. Felise was on the look-out for them, and opened the door softly before they had time to knock.

'Come in,' she whispered. 'My father is asleep upstairs, and we must not wake him. I have made coffee for you in here.'

She led the way into a small cosy sitting-room. A spirit lamp stood in the grate, and bending over it, she brewed them both some fragrant coffee.

Then Jack unfastened the Chinese jar from its many wrappings. Felise gasped as her eyes fell on it.

'But yes, but yes,' she cried eagerly. 'That is it – I would know it anywhere.'

Meanwhile Lavington was making his own preparations. He removed all the ornaments from a small table and set it in the middle of the room. Round it he placed three chairs. Then, taking the blue jar from Jack, he placed it in the centre of the table.

'Now,' he said, 'we are ready. Turn off the lights, and let us sit round the table in the darkness.'

The others obeyed him. Lavington's voice spoke again out of the darkness.

'Think of nothing – or of everything. Do not force the mind. It is possible that one of us has mediumistic powers. If so, that person will go into a trance. Remember, there is nothing to fear. Cast out fear from your hearts, and drift – drift——'

His voice died away and there was silence. Minute by minute, the silence seemed to grow more pregnant with possibilities. It was all very well for Lavington to say 'Cast our fear.' It was not fear that Jack felt – it was panic. And he was almost certain that Felise felt the same way. Suddenly he heard her voice, low and terrified.

'Something terrible is going to happen. I feel it.'

'Cast out fear,' said Lavington. 'Do not fight against the influence.'

The darkness seemed to get darker and the silence more acute. And nearer and nearer came that indefinable sense of menace.

Jack felt himself choking – stifling – the evil thing was very near. . . .

And then the moment of conflict passed. He was drifting, drifting down stream – his lids closed – peace – darkness. . . .

Jack stirred slightly. His head was heavy – heavy as lead. Where was he?

Sunshine . . . birds. . . . He lay staring up at the sky.

Then it all came back to him. The sitting. The little room. Felise and the doctor. What had happened?

He sat up, his head throbbing unpleasantly, and looked round him. He was lying in a little copse not far from the cottage. No one else was near him. He took out his watch. To his amazement it registered half past twelve.

Jack struggled to his feet, and ran as far as he could in the direction of the cottage. They must have been alarmed by his failure to come out of the trance, and carried him out into the open air.

Arrived at the cottage, he knocked loudly on the door. But there was no answer, and no signs of life about it. They must have gone off to get help. Or else – Jack felt an indefinable fear invade him. What had happened last night?

He made his way back to the hotel as quickly as possible. He was about to make some inquiries at the office, when he was diverted by a colossal punch in the ribs which nearly knocked him off his feet. Turning in some indignation, he beheld a white-haired old gentleman wheezing with mirth.

'Didn't expect me, my boy. Didn't expect me, hey?' said this individual.

'Why, Uncle George, I thought you were miles away – in Italy somewhere.'

'Ah! but I wasn't. Landed at Dover last night. Thought I'd motor up to town and stop here to see you on the way.

And what did I find. Out all night, hey? Nice goings on——'

'Uncle George,' Jack checked him firmly. 'I've got the most extraordinary story to tell you. I dare say you won't believe it.'

'I dare say I shan't,' laughed the old man. 'But do your best, my boy.'

'But I must have something to eat,' continued Jack. 'I'm famished.'

He led the way to the dining-room, and over a substantial repast, he narrated the whole story.

'And God knows what's become of them,' he ended.

His uncle seemed on the verge of apoplexy.

'The jar,' he managed to ejaculate at last. 'THE BLUE JAR! What's become of that?'

Jack stared at him in non-comprehension, but submerged in the torrent of words that followed he began to understand.

It came with a rush: 'Ming – unique – gem of my collection – worth ten thousand pounds at least – offer from Hoggenheimer, the American millionaire – only one of its kind in the world – Confound it, sir, what have you done with my BLUE JAR?'

Jack rushed from the room. He must find Lavington. The young lady at the office eyed him coldly.

'Dr Lavington left late last night – by motor. He left a note for you.'

Jack tore it open. It was short and to the point.

MY DEAR YOUNG FRIEND,

Is the day of the supernatural over? Not quite – especially when tricked out in new scientific language. Kindest regards from Felise, invalid father, and myself. We have twelve hours start, which ought to be ample.

Yours ever,

AMBROSE LAVINGTON,

Doctor of the Soul.

The Manhood of Edward Robinson

'With a swing of his mighty arms, Bill lifted her right off her feet, crushing her to his breast. With a deep sigh she yielded her lips in such a kiss as he had never dreamed of——'

With a sigh, Mr Edward Robinson put down *Where Love is King* and stared out of the window of the underground train. They were running through Stamford Brook. Edward Robinson was thinking about Bill. Bill was the real hundred per cent he-man beloved of lady novelists. Edward envied him his muscles, his rugged good looks, and his terrific passions. He picked up the book again and read the description of the proud Marchesa Bianca (she who had yielded her lips). So ravishing was her beauty, the intoxication of her was so great, that strong men went down before her like ninepins, faint and helpless with love.

'Of course,' said Edward to himself, 'it's all bosh, this sort of stuff. All bosh, it is. And yet, I wonder——'

His eyes looked wistful. Was there such a thing as a world of romance and adventure somewhere? Were there women whose beauty intoxicated? Was there such a thing as love that devoured one like a flame?

'This is real life, this is,' said Edward. 'I've got to go on the same just like all the other chaps.'

On the whole, he supposed, he ought to consider himself a lucky young man. He had an excellent berth – clerkship in a flourishing concern. He had good health, no one dependant upon him, and he was engaged to Maud.

But the mere thought of Maud brought a shadow over his face. Though he would never have admitted it, he was afraid of Maud. He loved her – yes – he still remembered the thrill with which he had admired the back of her white neck rising out of the cheap four and elevenpenny blouse on the first occasion they had met. He had sat behind her at the cinema, and the friend he was with had known her and had introduced them. No doubt about it, Maud was very superior. She was good-looking and clever and very lady-like, and she was always right about everything. The kind of girl, every one said, who would make such an excellent wife.

Edward wondered whether the Marchesa Bianca would have made an excellent wife. Somehow, he doubted it. He couldn't picture the voluptuous Bianca, with her red lips and her swaying form, tamely sewing on buttons, say, for the virile Bill. No, Bianca was Romance, and this was real life. He and Maud would be very happy together. She had so much common sense. . . .

But all the same, he wished that she wasn't quite so – well, sharp in manner. So prone to 'jump upon him.'

It was, of course, her prudence and her common sense which made her do so. Maud was very sensible. And, as a rule, Edward was very sensible too, but sometimes—— He had wanted to get married this Christmas, for instance. Maud had pointed out how much more prudent it would be to wait a while – a year or two, perhaps. His salary was not large. He had wanted to give her an expensive ring – she had been horror stricken, and had forced him to take it back and exchange it for a cheaper one. Her qualities were all excellent qualities, but sometimes Edward wished that she had more faults and less virtues. It was her virtues that drove him to desperate deeds.

For instance——

A blush of guilt overspread his face. He had got to tell her –

and tell her soon. His secret guilt was already making him behave strangely. Tomorrow was the first of three days holiday, Christmas Eve, Christmas Day and Boxing Day. She had suggested that he should come round and spend the day with her people, and in a clumsy foolish manner, a manner that could not fail to arouse her suspicions, he had managed to get out of it – had told a long, lying story about a pal of his in the country with whom he had promised to spend the day.

And there was no pal in the country. There was only his guilty secret.

Three months ago, Edward Robinson, in company with a few hundred thousand other young men, had gone in for a competition in one of the weekly papers. Twelve girls' names had to be arranged in order of popularity. Edward had had a brilliant idea. His own preference was sure to be wrong – he had noticed that in several similar competitions. He wrote down the twelve names arranged in his own order of merit, then he wrote them down again this time placing one from the top and one from the bottom of the list alternately.

When the result was announced, Edward had got eight right out of the twelve, and was awarded the first prize of £500. This result, which might easily be ascribed to luck, Edward persisted in regarding as the direct outcome of his 'system.' He was inordinately proud of himself.

The next thing was, what to do with the £500? He knew very well what Maud would say. Invest it. A nice little nest egg for the future. And, of course, Maud would be quite right, he knew that. But to win money as the result of a competition is an entirely different feeling from anything else in the world.

Had the money been left to him as a legacy, Edward would have invested it religiously in Conversion Loan or Savings Certificates as a matter of course. But money that one has achieved by a mere stroke of the pen, by a lucky and unbelievable chance, comes under the same heading as a child's sixpence – 'for your very own – to spend as you like.'

And in a certain rich shop which he passed daily on his way to the office, was the unbelievable dream, a small two-seater car, with a long shining nose, and the price clearly displayed on it – £465.

'If I were rich,' Edward had said to it, day after day. 'If I were rich, I'd have you.'

And now he was – if not rich – at least possessed of a lump sum of money sufficient to realize his dream. That car, that shining alluring piece of loveliness, was his if he cared to pay the price.

He had meant to tell Maud about the money. Once he had told her, he would have secured himself against temptation. In face of Maud's horror and disapproval, he would never have the courage to persist in his madness. But, as it chanced, it was Maud herself who clinched the matter. He had taken her to the cinema – and to the best seats in the house. She had pointed out to him, kindly but firmly, the criminal folly of his behaviour – wasting good money – three and sixpence against two and fourpence, when one saw just as well from the latter places.

Edward took her reproaches in sullen silence. Maud felt contentedly that she was making an impression. Edward could not be allowed to continue in these extravagant ways. She loved Edward, but she realized that he was weak – hers the task of being ever at hand to influence him in the way he should go. She observed his worm-like demeanour with satisfaction.

Edward was indeed worm-like. Like worms, he turned. He remained crushed by her words, but it was at that precise minute that he made up his mind to buy the car.

'Damn it,' said Edward to himself. 'For once in my life, I'll do what I like. Maud can go hang!'

And the very next morning, he had walked into that palace of plate glass, with its lordly inmates in their glory of gleaming enamel and shimmering metal, and with an insoucIance that surprised himself, he bought the car. It was the easiest thing in the world, buying a car!

It had been his for four days now. He had gone about, outwardly calm, but inwardly bathed in ecstasy. And to Maud he had as yet breathed no word. For four days, in his luncheon hour, he had received instruction in the handling of the lovely creature. He was an apt pupil.

Tomorrow, Christmas Eve, he was to take her out into the country. He had lied to Maud, and he would lie again if need be. He was enslaved body and soul by his new possession. It stood to him for Romance, for Adventure, for all the things that he had longed for and had never had. Tomorrow, he and his mistress would take the road together. They would rush through the keen cold air, leaving the throb and fret of London far behind them – out into the wide clear spaces. . . .

At this moment, Edward, though he did not know it, was very near to being a poet.

Tomorrow——

He looked down at the book in his hand – *When Love is King*. He laughed and stuffed it into his pocket. The car, and the red lips of the Marchesa Bianca, and the amazing prowess of Bill seemed all mixed up together. Tomorrow——

The weather, usually a sorry jade to those who count upon her, was kindly disposed towards Edward. She gave him the day of his dreams, a day of glittering frost, and pale-blue sky, and a primrose-yellow sun.

So, in a mood of high adventure, a dare-devil wickedness, Edward drove out of London. There was trouble at Hyde Park Corner, and a sad *contretemps* at Putney Bridge, there was much protesting of gears, and a frequent jarring of brakes, and much abuse was freely showered upon Edward by the drivers of other vehicles. But for a novice he did not acquit himself so badly, and presently he came out on to one of those fair wide roads that are the joy of the motorist. There was little congestion on this particular road today. Edward drove on and on, drunk with his mastery over this creature of the gleaming sides, speeding through the cold white world with the elation of a god.

It was a delirious day. He stopped for lunch at an old-fashioned inn, and again later for tea. Then reluctantly he turned homewards – back again to London, to Maud, to the inevitable explanation, recriminations. . . .

He shook off the thought with a sigh. Let tomorrow look after itself. He still had today. And what could be more fascinating than this? Rushing through the darkness with the headlights searching out the way in front. Why, this was the best of all!

He judged that he had no time to stop anywhere for dinner. This driving through the darkness was a ticklish business. It was going to take longer to get back to London than he had thought. It was just eight o'clock when he passed through Hindhead and came out upon the rim of the Devil's Punch Bowl. There was moonlight, and the snow that had fallen two days ago was still unmelted.

He stopped the car and stood staring. What did it matter if he didn't get back to London until midnight? What did it matter if he never got back? He wasn't going to tear himself away from this all at once.

He got out of the car, and approached the edge. There was a path winding down temptingly near him. Edward yielded to the spell. For the next half-hour he wandered deliriously in a snowbound world. Never had he imagined anything quite like this. And it was his, his very own, given to him by his shining mistress who waited for him faithfully on the road above.

He climbed up again, got into the car and drove off, still a little dizzy from that discovery of sheer beauty which comes to the most prosaic men once in a while.

Then, with a sigh, he came to himself, and thrust his hand into the pocket of the car where he had stuffed an additional muffler earlier in the day.

But the muffler was no longer there. The pocket was

empty. No, not completely empty – there was something scratchy and hard – like pebbles.

Edward thrust his hand deep down. In another minute he was staring like a man bereft of his senses. The object that he held in his hand, dangling from his fingers, with the moonlight striking a hundred fires from it, was a diamond necklace.

Edward stared and stared. But there was no doubting possible. A diamond necklace worth probably thousands of pounds (for the stones were large ones) had been casually reposing in the side-pocket of the car.

But who had put it there? It had certainly not been there when he started from town. Some one must have come along when he was walking about in the snow, and deliberately thrust it in. But why? Why choose *his* car? Had the owner of the necklace made a mistake? Or was it – could it possibly be – a *stolen* necklace?

And then, as all these thoughts went whirling through his brain, Edward suddenly stiffened and went cold all over. *This was not his car.*

It was very like it, yes. It was the same brilliant shade of scarlet – red as the Marchesa Bianca's lips – it had the same long and gleaming nose, but by a thousand small signs, Edward realized that it was not his car. Its shining newness was scarred here and there, it bore signs, faint but unmistakable, of wear and tear. In that case . . .

Edward, without more ado, made haste to turn the car. Turning was not his strong point. With the gear in reverse, he invariably lost his head and twisted the wheel the wrong way. Also, he frequently became entangled between the accelerator and the foot brake with disastrous results. In the end, however, he succeeded, and straight away the car began purring up the hill again.

Edward remembered that there had been another car standing some little distance away. He had not noticed it particularly at the time. He had returned from his walk by a different path from that by which he had gone down in the hollow. This second path had brought him out on the road immediately behind, as he had thought, his own car. It must really have been the other one.

In about ten minutes he was once more at the spot where he had halted. But there was now no car at all by the roadside. Whoever had owned this car must now have gone off in Edward's – he also, perhaps, misled by the resemblance.

Edward took out the diamond necklace from his pocket and let it run through his fingers perplexedly.

What to do next? Run on to the nearest police station? Explain the circumstances, hand over the necklace, and give the number of his own car.

By the by, what was the number of his car? Edward thought and thought, but for the life of him he couldn't remember. He felt a cold sinking sensation. He was going to look the most utter fool at the police station. There was an eight in it, that was all that he could remember. Of course, it didn't really matter – at least . . . He looked uncomfortably at the diamonds. Supposing they should think – oh, but they wouldn't – and yet again they might – that he had stolen the car and the diamonds? Because, after all, when one came to think of it, would any one in their senses thrust a valuable diamond necklace carelessly into the open pocket of a car?

Edward got out and went round to the back of the motor. Its number was XRI0061. Beyond the fact that that was certainly not the number of his car, it conveyed nothing to him. Then he set to work systematically to search all the pockets. In the one where he had found the diamonds he made a discovery – a small scrap of paper with some words pencilled on it. By the light of the headlights, Edward read them easily enough.

'Meet me, Greane, corner of Salter's Lane, ten o'clock.'

He remembered the name Greane. He had seen it on a sign-post earlier in the day. In a minute, his mind was made up. He would go to this village, Greane, find Salter's Lane, meet the person who had written the note, and explain the circumstances. That would be much better than looking a fool in the local police station.

He started off almost happily. After all, this was an adventure. This was the sort of thing that didn't happen every day. The diamond necklace made it exciting and mysterious.

He had some little difficulty in finding Greane, and still more difficulty in finding Salter's Lane, but after knocking up two cottages, he succeeded.

Still, it was a few minutes after the appointed hour when he drove cautiously along a narrow road, keeping a sharp look out on the left-hand side where he had been told Salter's Lane branched off.

He came upon it quite suddenly round a bend, and even as he drew up, a figure came forward out of the darkness.

'At last!' a girl's voice cried. 'What an age you've been, Gerald!'

As she spoke, the girl stepped right into the glare of the headlights, and Edward caught his breath. She was the most glorious creature he had ever seen.

She was quite young, with hair black as night, and wonderful scarlet lips. The heavy cloak that she wore swung open, and Edward saw that she was in full evening dress – a kind of flame-coloured sheath, outling her perfect body. Round her neck was a row of exquisite pearls.

Suddenly the girl started.

'Why,' she cried; 'it isn't Gerald.'

'No,' said Edward hastily. 'I must explain.' He took the diamond necklace from his pocket and held it out to her. 'My name is Edward——'

He got no further, for the girl clapped her hands and broke in:

'Edward, of course! I am so glad. But that idiot Jimmy told me over the phone that he was sending Gerald along with the car. It's awfully sporting of you to come. I've been dying to meet you. Remember I haven't seen you since I was six years old. I see you've got the necklace all right. Shove it in your pocket again. The village policeman might come along and see it. Brrr, it's cold as ice waiting here! Let me get in.'

As though in a dream Edward opened the door, and she sprang lightly in beside him. Her furs swept his cheek, and an elusive scent, like that of violets after rain, assailed his nostrils.

He had no plan, no definite thought even. In a minute, without conscious volition, he had yielded himself to the adventure. She had called him Edward – what matter if he were the wrong Edward? She would find him out soon enough. In the meantime, let the game go on. He let in the clutch and they glided off.

Presently the girl laughed. Her laugh was just as wonderful as the rest of her.

'It's easy to see you don't know much about cars. I suppose they don't have them out there?'

'I wonder where "out there" is?' thought Edward. Aloud he said, 'Not much.'

'Better let me drive,' said the girl. 'It's tricky work finding your way round these lanes until we get on the main road again.'

He relinquished his place to her gladly. Presently they were humming through the night at a pace and with a recklessness that secretly appalled Edward. She turned her head towards him.

'I like pace. Do you? You know – you're not a bit like Gerald. No one would ever take you to be brothers. You're not a bit like what I imagined, either.'

'I suppose,' said Edward, 'that I'm so completely ordinary. Is that it?'

'Not ordinary – different. I can't make you out. How's poor old Jimmy? Very fed up, I suppose?'

'Oh, Jimmy's all right,' said Edward.

'It's easy enough to say that – but it's rough luck on him having a sprained ankle. Did he tell you the whole story?'

'Not a word. I'm completely in the dark. I wish you'd enlighten me.'

'Oh, the thing worked like a dream. Jimmy went in at the front door, togged up in his girl's clothes. I gave him a minute or two, and then skinned up to the window. Agnes Larella's maid was there laying out Agnes's dress and jewels, and all the rest. Then there was a great yell downstairs, and the squib went off, and every one shouted fire. The maid dashed out, and I hopped in, helped myself to the necklace, and was out and down in a flash, and out of the place the back way across the Punch Bowl. I shoved the necklace and the notice where to pick me up in the pocket of the car in passing. Then I joined Louise at the hotel, having shed my snow boots of course. Perfect *alibi* for me. She'd no idea I'd been out at all.'

'And what about Jimmy?'

'Well, you know more about that than I do.'

'He didn't tell me anything,' said Edward easily.

'Well, in the general rag, he caught his foot in his skirt and managed to sprain it. They had to carry him to the car, and the Larellas' chauffeur drove him home. Just fancy if the chauffeur had happened to put his hand in the pocket!'

Edward laughed with her, but his mind was busy. He understood the position more or less now. The name of Larella was vaguely familiar to him – it was a name that spelt wealth. This girl, and an unknown man called Jimmy, had conspired together to steal the necklace, and had succeeded. Owing to his sprained ankle and the presence of the Larellas' chauffeur Jimmy had not been able to look in the pocket of the car before telephoning the girl – probably had had no wish to do so. But it was almost certain that the other unknown 'Gerald' would do so at any early opportunity. And in it, he would find Edward's muffler!

A tram flashed past them, they were on the outskirts of

London. They flashed in and out of the traffic. Edward's heart stood in his mouth. She was a wonderful driver, this girl, but she took risks!

Quarter of an hour later they drew up before an imposing house in a frigid square.

'We can shed some of our clothing here,' said the girl, 'before we go on to Ritson's.'

'Ritson's?' queried Edward. He mentioned the famous night-club almost reverently.

'Yes, didn't Gerald tell you?'

'He did not,' said Edward grimly. 'What about my clothes.'

She frowned.

'Didn't they tell you *anything*? We'll rig you up somehow. We've got to carry this through.'

A stately butler opened the door and stood aside to let them enter.

'Mr Gerald Champneys rang up, your ladyship. He was very anxious to speak to you, but he wouldn't leave a message.'

'I bet he was anxious to speak to her,' said Edward to himself. 'At any rate, I know my full name now. Edward Champneys. But who is she? Your ladyship, they called her. What does she want to steal a necklace for? Bridge debts?'

In the *feuilletons* which he occasionally read, the beautiful and titled heroine was always driven desperate by bridge debts.

Edward was led away by the stately butler, and delivered over to a smooth-mannered valet. A quarter of an hour later he rejoined his hostess in the hall, exquisitely attired in evening clothes made in Saville Row which fitted him to a nicety.

Heavens! What a night!

They drove in the car to the famous Ritson's. In common with every one else Edward had read scandalous paragraphs concerning Ritson's. Any one who was any one turned up at

Ritson's sooner or later. Edward's only fear was that some one who knew the real Edward Champneys might turn up. He consoled himself by the reflection that the real man had evidently been out of England for some years.

Sitting at a little table against the wall, they sipped cocktails. Cocktails! To the simple Edward they represented the quintessence of the fast life. The girl, wrapped in a wonderful embroidered shawl, sipped nonchalantly. Suddenly she dropped the shawl from her shoulders and rose.

'Let's dance.'

Now the one thing Edward could do to perfection was to dance. When he and Maud took the floor together at the Palaise de Danse, lesser lights stood still and watched in admiration.

'I nearly forgot,' said the girl suddenly. 'The necklace?'

She held out her hand. Edward, completely bewildered, drew it from his pocket and gave it to her. To his utter amazement, she coolly clasped it round her neck. Then she smiled up at him intoxicatingly.

'Now,' she said softly, 'we'll dance.'

They danced. And in all Ritson's nothing more perfect could be seen.

Then, as at length they returned to their table, an old gentleman with a would-be rakish air accosted Edward's companion.

'Ah! Lady Noreen, always dancing! Yes, yes. Is Captain Folliot here tonight?'

'Jimmy's taken a toss – racked his ankle.'

'You don't say so? How did that happen?'

'No details as yet.'

She laughed and passed on.

Edward followed, his brain in a whirl. He knew now. Lady Noreen Elliot, the famous Lady Noreen herself, perhaps the most talked of girl in England. Celebrated for her beauty, for her daring – the leader of that set known as the Bright Young People. Her engagement to Captain James Folliot, V.C., of the Household Cavalry, had been recently announced.

But the necklace? He still couldn't understand the necklace. He must risk giving himself away, but know he must.

As they sat down again, he pointed to it.

'Why that, Noreen?' he said. 'Tell me why?'

She smiled dreamily, her eyes far away, the spell of the dance still holding her.

'It's difficult for you to understand, I suppose. One gets so tired of the same thing – always the same thing. Treasure hunts were all very well for a while, but one gets used to everything. "Burglaries" were my idea. Fifty pounds entrance fee, and lots to be drawn. This is the third. Jimmy and I drew Agnes Larella. You know the rules? Burglary to be carried out within three days and the loot to be worn for at least an hour in a public place, or you forfeit your stake and a hundred-pound fine. It's rough luck on Jimmy spraining his ankle, but we'll scoop the pool all right.'

'I see,' said Edward, drawing a deep breath. 'I see.'

Noreen rose suddenly, pulling her shawl round her.

'Drive me somewhere in the car. Down to the docks. Somewhere horrible and exciting. Wait a minute——' She reached up and unclasped the diamonds from her neck. 'You'd better take these again. I don't want to be murdered for them.'

They went out of Ritson's together. The car stood in a small by-street, narrow and dark. As they turned the corner towards it, another car drew up to the curb, and a young man sprang out.

'Thank the Lord, Noreen, I've got hold of you at last,' he cried. 'There's the devil to pay. That ass Jimmy got off with the wrong car. God knows where those diamonds are at this minute. We're in the devil of a mess.'

Lady Noreen stared at him.

'What do you mean? We've got the diamonds – at least Edward has.'

'Edward?'

'Yes.' She made a slight gesture to indicate the figure by her side.

'It's I who am in the devil of a mess,' thought Edward. 'Ten to one this is brother Gerald.'

The young man stared at him.

'What do you mean?' he said slowly. 'Edward's in Scotland.'

'Oh!' cried the girl. She stared at Edward. 'Oh!'

Her colour came and went.

'So you,' she said, in a low voice, 'are the real thing?'

It took Edward just one minute to grasp the situation. There was awe in the girl's eyes – was it, could it be – admiration? Should he explain? Nothing so tame! He would play up to the end.

He bowed ceremoniously.

'I have to thank you, Lady Noreen,' he said, in the best highwayman manner, 'for a most delightful evening.'

One quick look he cast at the car from which the other had just alighted. A scarlet car with a shining bonnet. His car!

'And I will wish you good evening.'

One quick spring and he was inside, his foot on the clutch. The car started forward. Gerald stood paralyzed, but the girl was quicker. As the car slid past she leapt for it, alighting on the running board.

The car swerved, shot blindly round the corner and pulled up. Noreen, still panting from her spring, laid her hand on Edward's arm.

'You must give it me – oh, you must give it me. I've got to return it to Agnes Larella. Be a sport – we've had a good evening together – we've danced – we've been – pals. Won't you give it to me? To *me*?'

A woman who intoxicated you with her beauty. There were such women then. . . .

Also, Edward was only too anxious to get rid of the necklace. It was a heaven-sent opportunity for a *beau geste*.

He took it from his pocket and dropped it into her outstretched hand.

'We've been – pals,' he said.

'Ah!' Her eyes smouldered – lit up.

Then surprisingly she bent her head to him. For a moment he held her, her lips against his. . . .

Then she jumped off. The scarlet car sped forward with a great leap.

Romance!

Adventure!

At twelve o'clock on Christmas Day, Edward Robinson strode into the tiny drawing-room of a house in Clapham, with the customary greeting of 'Merry Christmas.'

Maud, who was rearranging a piece of holly, greeted him coldly.

'Have a good day in the country with that friend of yours?' she inquired.

'Look here,' said Edward. 'That was a lie I told you. I won a competition – £500, and I bought a car with it. I didn't tell you because I knew you'd kick up a row about it. That's the first thing. I've bought the car and there's nothing more to be said about it. The second thing is this – I'm not going to hang about for years. My prospects are quite good enough and I mean to marry you next month. See?'

'Oh!' said Maud faintly.

Was this – could this be – *Edward* speaking in this masterful fashion?

'Will you?' said Edward. 'Yes or no?'

She gazed at him, fascinated. There was awe and admiration in her eyes, and the sight of that look was intoxicating to Edward. Gone was that patient motherliness which had roused him to exasperation.

So had the Lady Noreen looked at him last night. But the Lady Noreen had receded far away, right into the region of Romance, side by side with the Marchesa Bianca. This was the Real Thing. This was his woman.

'Yes or no?' he repeated, and drew a step nearer.

'Ye – ye-es,' faltered Maud. 'But, oh, Edward, what has happened to you? You're quite different today.'

'Yes,' said Edward. 'For twenty-four hours I've been a man instead of a worm – and, by God, it pays!'

He caught her in his arms almost as Bill the superman might have done.

'Do you love me, Maud? Tell me, do you love me?'

'Oh, Edward!' breathed Maud. 'I adore you. . . .'